THE WIPE

Author's dedication:

For my lockdown family, Dan, Lily and Jack, for helping to keep me sane.

THE WIPE

Nik Abnett

NewCon Press
England

First published in April 2021 by NewCon Press,
41 Wheatsheaf Road, Alconbury Weston, Cambs, PE28 4LF

NCP257 (limited edition hardback)
NCP258 (softback)

10 9 8 7 6 5 4 3 2 1

ISBN:

978-1-912950-82-9 (hardback)
978-1-912950-83-6 (softback)

Cover by Ben Baldwin

Text edited by Ian Whates
Typesetting and interior layout by Ian Whates

One

Dharma Tuke crossed the lobby of her building and stepped over the threshold into the wipe.

She lived on the sixth floor, but the lifts had been taken out during the Deluge: too many people, too close together. She didn't mind the stairs, because she loved her comfortable apartment. She had large rooms and the ceilings were high. She even had a separate bedroom and kitchen. The bathroom was three times the size of its wipe.

The lobby doors closed behind her, and she reminded herself to order a new canister for her bathroom wipe.

If she'd ever smelled a geranium, she'd know that was the scent that surrounded her in the closed space for the few seconds that she stood in it, waiting for the exterior doors to slide open.

One of the nicer aspects of her building was that the internal doors were acrylic and see-through, so if she felt claustrophobic she could see into the lobby of the building. She'd hated closed spaces as a child, and had sometimes screamed, alone in the darkness, trapped in the wipe of her mother's building. She'd grown out of it. Still, it was nice to be able to see space for those few seconds; all she had to do was turn around. She almost never did.

The solid exterior doors slid open in front of her, and Dharma walked out into the street.

Five minutes later, she took a cup of coffee from the machine outside her office building, holding it in her gloved hand until she had passed through its wipe. She'd run late that morning and skipped breakfast, so she was really looking forward to that first sip of coffee.

The smell of ozone wafted around Dharma. A moment later, she stepped through the interior door, and waited for it to close behind her before taking that first sip. It did not disappoint.

The concierge, sitting at his desk in the lobby, smiled at her, and she raised a hand to him in greeting. They had never spoken, but the little human contact, at a distance of four or five metres, was always welcome. Dharma had never thought about why he was there, because he never seemed to do anything but sit behind his empty desk and smile at her. She had no digital connection to him, but had never wondered whether anyone else in the building had, or whether he was of any practical use to anyone. She didn't even know his name.

It was two flights of stairs up to Dharma's floor. She took them easily. Since the Deluge, buildings had never been built higher than three storeys. But many of the old buildings remained. Money had been better spent on other projects, but all the lifts had gone, no matter the height of the building. Her mother had told her about them once, when Dharma had been a child, and had complained about the five flights of stairs up to their apartment.

"You're too big to be carried, any more," her mother had said. "You'll have to get used to it, just as I had to get used to it when I was your age. Your grandmother used to talk about the lifts she used when she was a child, and buses, too, but the Deluge ended all that."

She remembered the conversation, but it had all happened so long ago she wondered whether it was within anyone's living memory. If it was, she wondered what those memories might be, and how accurate.

History downloads were better. They told the truth about the Deluge. That's how she'd learned about it, sitting in her mother's apartment, downloading school.

It didn't matter. Life was as it was, and she was living it in contentment.

Dharma passed through the wipe to her floor, the last before she could get on with her day. There was a rubber seal on the door to her cubicle, so that clean air could be circulated within, and the door closed behind her, using a simple cable and weight.

All the cubicles on Dharma's floor were singles, so all the maintenance had to be done by the occupants. Dharma had fitted a new cable to the hook above the door, and to the weight, when the old one had become frayed a couple of years ago.

She took off her coat and gloves, shoved the gloves in the coat pocket, and hung it on the back of the door.

She sat at her desk.

One wall of the cubicle was made of a thick, discoloured acrylic which had become scuffed with age, but it allowed her to see out of her cubicle. She could see others coming and going, and she could partly see into several other cubicles if she looked at an angle. There was no light in her cubicle, except for what came in through the acrylic wall, so everything had a slight green colour cast: the white walls, sealed concrete floor, acrylic desk and chair, even the steel hook on the back of her door. Her blue coat was not quite as blue as it had seemed outside.

Others on her floor had replaced their original walls; the new ones were more transparent, and less green, but Dharma liked the softness of hers, and didn't plan to change it any time soon.

Dharma had been working for Willoughby Woolman for six years, four of them in her current cubicle, but, like everyone else, she worked remotely. Her acquaintances in the building, the people she saw coming and going and anyone she encountered outside, worked in their own cubicles for other companies. She had never met another data-analyst for Willoughby Woolman, or anyone else who worked for them. It didn't matter.

Dharma put her face close to the sensor on her computer, and blinked. The screen came to life.

She was one of the lucky ones. Her computing power was above average, and she had good access to the company intranet, and to parts of the internet. She also had capacity for five private connections, which could not be monitored by W.W.

It was a condition of her solitariness. Cubicles of two, three or even four, had the same computing capacity as her cubicle. They were required to share, but Dharma had the advantage of being a single user.

She knew, of course, that her private connections could be monitored; she wasn't naive. But W.W. contracted not to monitor her, and she trusted that.

Dharma's computer logged on automatically to Willoughby Woolman's intranet home page. She mouthed her passcode at the sensor. She had VR, but W.W. preferred this security measure. The cubicles were not soundproof, but when she was sitting at her station she had her back to the acrylic wall, so no one could read her lips.

The passcode took Dharma to her personal schedule first, and then to feedback on her current project.

Everything was looking good; there were some small adjustments needed from the extra data provided, but it all made perfect sense to her. This would be an easy day. All those years downloading school in her mother's apartment had paid off. Her qualifications put her in the ninetieth percentile of the population. Education had its perks.

Dharma started working through the data, making the adjustments verbally through voice recognition, and seeing the screen scrolling in front of her as her notes were added to the analysis. She'd be done in a couple of hours, maybe less.

Two

Blythe Dole remembered her first encounter with Dharma Tuke. It had mesmerised her then, and it mesmerised her still.

It had been several months after she had first had a request from Dharma, before she was able to allocate one of her private connections to their relationship. Dharma and Blythe could speak two weeks out of three. Blythe was hard-wired into her service connection, and she couldn't give up her primary connection to her mother. It didn't matter very much to her, but if she altered the connection Blythe's mother would never let her hear the end of it.

Blythe's cubicle had two other occupants, and the three of them all worked for Anley Corp. Mostly, the work was dull and impenetrable. She didn't understand the invoices that she generated on behalf of the company. She could calculate the rates for various services, apply the discounts and add the taxes in the right sequences, of course. Her work was almost never questioned or corrected, but the products and services that Anley Corp provided were given alpha-numeric codes, which were meaningless to Blythe. Anley Corp's customers all had alpha-numeric codes, too, so, although she knew many of them as repeat customers, she had no idea what products and services she was invoicing for, or who was accessing them. Sometimes, she wished that she knew; sometimes she thought it was safer for her that she didn't.

Blythe's computing capacity was barely sufficient to her needs, because she had to share it with two other Anley Corp workers. It meant that she had to key in every character, so she spent long hours of her working day sitting at her computer station. If she had voice recognition, she could at least stand, stretch, and walk around a little, a very little in the confines of the cubicle. On the other hand, she had company, at least in theory.

Con sat adjacent to her on her left. He had introduced himself as Concord Penn when she had joined the cubicle three years earlier, but Joy Yardley, who sat on her other side always called him 'Con'.

The two of them were friendly, friendlier than Blythe thought they should be. Con and Joy would both rather speak to each other than to her. She knew their names but almost nothing else about them, except that 'Con' took his morning coffee with a double shot of hazelnut, which smelled too sweet and synthetic. It made Blythe think less of him than she might otherwise. Joy did not live up to her name. If there was anything to complain about, she was the first to open her mouth, and, too often, she chose to complain about Blythe.

Being in company all day should have been a benefit; it had been one of her reasons for applying for the job in the first place. It hadn't paid off. She had no real company here and her computing capacity was compromised. As a consequence of sharing the cubicle, Blythe also had to share the allocated private connections with two other people. Each of them had a dedicated service connection. She had a maximum of two usable connections, and for one week in three she only had one private connection. She also had to share the internet capacity.

Blythe had waited for Joy's fortnight's holiday, three months after Dharma had reached out to her, before acknowledging the private e-mail. While Joy was out of the cubicle, she and Con had split the single extra private connection they were allocated. Con had pulled rank and insisted on taking the extra connection for the first week, so Blythe waited until the second week of Joy's holiday. By the time she was able to connect with Dharma, she had worked herself up to a pitch of excitement that Con neither noticed nor cared about.

Con always left the building for lunch, and the cubicle was never supposed to be empty during working hours, giving Blythe a forty minute window of opportunity. She was determined to make the most of it.

She opened the precious extra private connection and began to write the e-mail that she had been composing in her head for weeks. She was hoping for an immediate reply, so she had to keep it brief; Dharma needed time to read and answer it during those forty minutes, so that they could have some kind of conversation. Blythe couldn't know what kind of computer access Dharma had, or whether they took the same lunch break. If not, she'd have to wait until tomorrow for a reply.

+This is Blyth,+ she typed. +Finally able to reply. Tell me about our bond.+

She paused for a moment, before hitting the send button, wondering whether her brief message was enough. Perhaps she could have been friendlier.

She hit the button. She'd planned the e-mail carefully, to give them time; it was pointless to hesitate.

Within a couple of minutes, Blythe's screen blinked, and filled with text. Before she read it, she e-mailed Dharma back:

+No VR, text only.+

She could type a hundred words a minute, but had no voice recognition, and Dharma could talk much faster than she could type, especially when excited, so the conversation would be a little one-sided. Blythe scanned the e-mail for the salient points.

Three

It was after Dharma's mother had died that she began to wonder what other relations she might have. She was alone in the world, alone in her apartment, alone in her cubicle. She was always on her own.

There were people around her, of course. There were people on the street, sometimes, and there were people on the other sides of the walls that always surrounded her. It wasn't a physical connection she was looking for, although she'd been lucky to have one with her mother for so long. What she really missed was the emotional connection, the shared history. She missed knowing what her mother would want to talk about; she missed being able to finish her sentences, and vice versa.

Dharma's mother had not always been an easy woman, and their relationship could sometimes be tense. Dharma wondered if it was because it was the only physical or emotional relationship either one of them had. Dharma had been born while her grandmother was still alive, so her mother always had a connection to someone. Perhaps that's why they had spoken every day, and perhaps that's why they had met every weekend. Dharma's mother would often complain that it was not enough contact, not secure enough a connection. Dharma had never questioned it.

Then her mother died, and Dharma had begun to understand why their relationship, their connection, had meant so very much to her. She felt that she had taken it too much for granted, and now it was gone, with nothing to fill the void it left.

Dharma had spent the majority of the past decade alone; she had grown used to it, but her mother had feared Dharma would be lonely after she was dead. She had spoken of it, often.

Dharma was lonely. She was also resourceful. Her quick, analytical mind soon settled on a solution to this lack in her life.

She had loved her mother, even when she resented her. She wanted someone to love again, and even someone to resent, a little, from time to time.

Dharma didn't remember her grandmother, but her mother spoke of her often, and it seemed to Dharma that she and her mother had maintained a similar bond. Dharma had no child of her own, nor any prospect of having one any time soon, but she must have blood relations out there somewhere.

Perhaps blood was the connection. It had kept her grandmother close to her mother, and it had kept her mother close to her.

She would look for more of their blood.

Since the Deluge, women had raised children alone. There was no such thing as the romantic relationship that her grandmother had apparently shared with her grandfather. Dharma had often thought that her grandmother had lied about their relationship, or, at the very least, exaggerated the details. She fondly remembered her mother's gloved touch, but could not imagine another's skin against her own, could not imagine being naked in the company of another person, and did not believe any of the stories, passed down from her grandmother, about the process she called 'sex'.

The state had controlled the population since the Deluge.

Dharma would not have to do very much to become eligible to have a child, but, knowing what the process entailed, she was not sure that she wanted one, or that she would ever want one.

Nevertheless, Dharma had determined that blood was the key. She must find someone she shared genetic material with.

Dharma began to use most of her out-of-hours time in her cubicle to trace her ancestry.

She had choices, but she also had questions. Knowing that both she and her mother were only children, her links were limited. She would begin by tracing her grandmother's family. She thought about it, and quickly drew several conclusions.

There were records from before the Deluge: Good records. Registers of birth, marriage and death had been kept for several hundred years, census records, too. She did not doubt the good intentions of the state in keeping the data, or in allowing access to it, but as she scrolled through facsimiles of the kinds of records she would be able to find, she began to question their reliability.

She looked at the fields in the old twentieth century records. Birth certificates were registered by region, and were numbered with table references. Dharma assumed that meant there were paper records, books of information rather than clean, digital data. They must, surely, be riddled with human error. It was a serious concern.

The facsimile she downloaded showed a certificate with data across the top, including application number, registration district, year, sub-district and county, some of which Dharma did not understand. Then the body of the certificate was divided into columns, labelled: no; when and where born; name, if any; sex; name and surname of father; name, surname and maiden surname of mother; occupation of father; signature, description and residence of informant; when registered; signature of registrar; name entered after registration.

Dharma brought her skills in data analysis to bear, and came to a number of conclusions. Her biggest concern was the column headed 'signature, description and residence of informant'. What had qualified a person to be an informant of a birth? Dharma left the tab open, and searched, randomly, for visuals of genuine artefact birth certificates. There appeared to be a great many in the public domain. She went from one to another, but found very little variation. In most instances, it appeared that the informant for the birth of a child was its father. When not the father, it was generally the mother.

She also noticed that up to six weeks could pass between the date of the child's birth and the date of its registration.

Dharma was concerned that she could trust very little from the twentieth century certificates that she was able to view, and she could find no evidence of any state authority verifying the births.

She knew little about how children had once been conceived, except that it was by a physical act between a man and a woman. Surely, any woman could accomplish this act with any man, and yet it was, so often, the fathers who informed the authorities of the birth of the child. It presumed that the father was, in-fact, genetically related to the child he was registering.

It seemed to Dharma that the freedom of physical contact between people that had been allowed in the twentieth century meant that no man could be confident that he was the genetic parent of any child. Of course, she was relying on her grandmother's second-hand stories, filtered through her mother, and they might just be myths. She couldn't know for sure.

These days things were much neater. Sperm was delivered to compatible, eligible women, selected to provide the strongest genetic combinations for the best chance of producing robust children. It was the reason Dharma had borne little physical resemblance to her mother. Her skin was brown, where her mothers had been pale; her eyes were a dark hazel while her mother's had been grey, and her hair kinked and curled while her mother's had been fair and straight and shiny. In fact, Dharma had not seen anyone as pale as her mother for a very long time.

It didn't matter, they had other things in common.

Dharma remembered, from downloading science school, that the human genome project had not been completed until early in the twenty-first century, only decades before the Deluge. She also remembered that accurate genetic testing for familial relationships had not been available until the 1980s. She did a quick calculation in her head and realised that, statistically, for the period from 1980 to the Deluge, the percentage of the population that was tested to prove the paternity of a child must be negligible.

In all but the rarest instances, the spouse of the pregnant woman simply assumed the child was his genetic offspring.

It wasn't good enough. There were no historic records that Dharma could rely on to find a blood relation on any male line.

Dharma would have to look at the women, if she was to trace any credible family members.

"But it's too long ago," she said, into thin air. She knew that her grandmother had been born on October 15th, but she didn't know what year. She knew that her name had been Verity Tuke. She got absolutely nowhere with her limited knowledge.

Dharma searched her memory for anything that her mother might have told her about her grandmother. She wished she could ask her but she couldn't, and her mother's medical, employment and domestic history, open to her for twelve months after her death, had now been sealed by the state, so she could no longer access it. She began to wish that she'd started her search sooner... Much, much sooner.

Dharma had not known her grandfather, only that her grandmother had told stories about him, and about their relationship, to her mother. Her mother had passed some of those stories on to Dharma, but Dharma hadn't taken much notice. She thought her mother told the stories to remember her own life, her own history, and her connections with the past before the Deluge. She wished that she could remember more of the details of those stories, and more about the people involved.

Dharma looked again at the facsimile certificate. She looked at the column marked 'name, surname and maiden surname of mother' it read, 'Jane Smith', and then, below, 'formerly Jones.' Then she looked back at the column marked 'name and surname of father'. It read, 'John Smith'. This fictional woman, the mother of this fictional child, had changed her surname to that of her fictional husband. All members of this fictional family carried one surname, that of the patriarch, 'John Smith'.

In the New Wave, children carried the same surname as their mothers. They had an identifying unique number for the sperm donor. That number appeared on Dharma's id, but she never gave it a thought. It was simply an alpha-numeric, and she saw hundreds of those every day in her work.

Dharma went back to the visuals of the genuine certificates, and found the same thing over and over again. For all the certificates where a child had both a mother and a father listed, the mother had adopted the father's surname. Perhaps her grandmother's name was not Verity Tuke, after all.

Dharma's grandmother had passed down lots of stories that made very little sense, some from before the Deluge and some from afterwards. It was the stories she had told about the two years, during the Deluge that were most confusing and surprising. They were the stories that Dharma had always doubted; they seemed so implausible.

Four

Verity was young when the Deluge began. She had been at university, studying for her first degree, when things started to change. Her father had demanded that she return home, before the restricted transport links were severed entirely.

"I can't come home, Pa. What about Sage?"

She'd been listening to her father for ten or fifteen minutes on their weekly Zoom call. She could see how angry he was, how determined that she must come home. At first, he'd tried being casual, tried cajoling her, tried to use her mum and her sister as leverage. None of it worked. None of the dozens of e-mails and texts he'd sent her during the past several weeks had worked, either.

Verity was in love with Sage, and she wouldn't leave him. There was no way for him to get home, since his parents lived overseas, and if she left him on campus and went home herself, she couldn't be sure that she'd ever see him again.

She was twenty-one; she could make her own decisions, and she chose to stay right where she was, with Sage.

"You're coming home!" her father said. "It's not safe. I've e-mailed your ticket already. Just use it."

Zoom had frozen for a moment as he finished speaking, and Verity was afraid that he'd signed off or, worse still, that the internet connection was down.

She was relieved when his face started to move, as he began to say something else. She cut him off.

"I know you want me to come home, Pa. I know Mum wants me to come home... I just... I just *can't*. I want to be with you, but I can't leave Sage."

"Boyfriends come and go. They're like buses... There'll be another one along in a minute."

"Buses!" said Verity. She could feel her face reddening and tears gather in the corners of her eyes. She didn't know what else to say.

17

Pa sighed, his presence large beside the small inset picture of her own miserable face. She knew that he was seeing the screen in reverse, that he would see how frightened and upset she was, that he would see her tears.

"Point taken," he said, and his face grew a little smaller on her screen as he slumped back in his seat. "My old sayings don't hold much water any more, do they?"

Verity shook her head. She couldn't speak, but swallowed hard on her tears, and sniffed.

"Okay," said Pa. "So, there aren't any more buses... You know that you still have to come home, though, right? If they shut down the campus, you'll have to leave, and, by then, you might not be able to get home."

"I know, Pa," said Verity, sniffing again.

"And you love him?"

"We've been together for two years, and I love him more every day. Mum was married by the time she was twenty-one, and you weren't much older."

"No, I wasn't much older."

They looked at each other for a few more moments.

"How about this," Pa finally said. "How about if I e-mail you a ticket for Sage, and he comes home with you?"

Verity held her breath for a moment, then said, "Can we do that? Do you think it's allowed?"

"He's been in the country the required length of time, and the campus infirmary can certificate him, if he passes their tests. Yes, it should be possible... But we have to do it right now, and if he doesn't pass the tests you have to promise me that you'll come home alone."

"If he doesn't pass the tests, what makes you think I'll pass them?" asked Verity.

"You'll pass them," said Pa. "You're a chip off the old block."

Verity wiped her eyes and smiled. Her father smiled back.

"Get to it. I'll sort that other ticket out right now."

"Thanks, Pa," said Verity. "Love you."

"You, too," he said, and Verity waved at her father as she hit the button to end the call.

Five

Dharma was more than a little thankful when she found open access to all pre-Deluge records. There had to be a way to find her grandmother. She hadn't been able to using the name Verity Tuke, but she knew that her husband's name was Sage, and that his surname was also Tuke. Perhaps she could track down his birth certificate.

In the back of her mind, Dharma couldn't help doubting the records, wondering whether Sage Tuke had really been her mother's genetic father. On the other hand, the Deluge lockdown had meant that families were isolated in their homes for long periods of time, and it might be difficult for her grandmother to speak to, let alone meet, or do the sex thing with someone else. According to her mother, Dharma's grandmother had liked sex, and if that were true, she might have done it with more than one man, but it would have been pretty difficult to find a way to do it during the time of the protocols.

"Mum first," she said, as she started speaking the details into the VR. "Connie Tuke, born 25th October 2042." The screen scrolled, and Dharma wondered whether she might need to give more information, especially as her mother had been born during the Deluge.

"Oh. Correction: Constance Tuke, born 25th October 2042."

The screen continued to scroll for several seconds, before flashing a data box.

+Data not found. Complete *Field+

"Show Field."

The field was headed +place of birth+.

Of course, Dharma had lived with her mother for the duration of her education. Part of the reason she had downloaded school for so long was because her mother couldn't bear their separation. Eventually the time had come when Dharma had to go out to work, her skill-set complete. They had lost their home and both been moved to single occupancy housing but, by then, Constance had senior status, so they could not be moved to the same building.

Dharma had made the best of her skills, so, she was able to ensure that they lived in the same district just three miles apart. It meant that she was permitted to visit her mother once a week, making the journey on-foot, without the need to pass through a quarantine wipe. Dharma had to take an apartment on the sixth floor of an old building, but she quickly got used to that, and she loved the extra space. Dharma was fit, and jogged the distance to her mother's in about thirty-five minutes, closer to forty if the weather was bad. She had even walked it several times in the snow, taking a little over an hour.

They were lucky, most adult children saw their elderly mothers, intermittently at best, and some never saw their mothers again once their education was over. Very few people could manipulate data the way that Dharma could.

Dharma knew exactly where she'd been born, in the same apartment that she'd grown up in. She didn't know for certain where her mother had been born, but was able to make an educated guess, and began with her own district.

"BRd1," she said.

A data box quickly appeared on the screen.

+Data not recognised+

Dharma stared at the data box for several moments. She didn't know what to try next, and, besides, her lunch break was coming to an end, and she had to log back into W.W.'s intranet home page.

She closed the internet connection, and went back to work.

The following day, having given the problem some thought, Dharma used her lunch break to look for old maps. She quickly discovered that maps from the Deluge were not in the public domain, and she doubted she could gain access via W.W. without a convincing reason for wanting them. Probably, better not to try.

Older maps *were* in the public domain. Dharma didn't know what had been changed since, or by how much, but it was worth a try. Most of the old maps she found were for the United Kingdom. She didn't recognise the name, but her first level of internet access was national.

Dharma pulled up a map at random, and said, "District field" into the VR.

+Data not recognised+

Dharma thought for a moment.

"Correction," she said. "Bromley."

Dharma had always called BRd1 her home, but her mother insisted on calling it Bromley.

The image zoomed in, with the header 'London Borough of Bromley'. She saw an irregular shaped green area with a red boundary. There were a number of lines, in various colours, some straight, others more like scribbles, running this way and that across the green area. There were also a number of grey, blocky patches, breaking up the green, with words printed across them.

One of these grey areas was labelled 'Bromley'. Others bore names like 'Orpington' and 'Downe'.

"Okay." She pulled up the tab for registration of births, and said, "Bromley," when the screen prompted +place of birth+.

She held her breath for a moment, and then read the data box.

+Data not found+

Dharma wasn't ready to give up.

"Correction: Downe," she said.

+Data not found+

By the time Dharma had corrected through all the grey patches in the London Borough of Bromley, she was several minutes late signing back into W.W.'s intranet, and she still hadn't found her mother's birth registration.

Undeterred, she decided to continue, no matter how long it took. Her mother had died almost two years ago, so time was already passing, but she had plenty more of it ahead of her. She had a good job, and a comfortable home, and she had lived without a significant emotional connection for all that time; she could wait a while longer. More than anything, Dharma had good access to the internet, and she knew how to search for and interpret data. If anyone could find a blood relation, Dharma knew that it was her.

New-wave records would probably not have begun until well after the Deluge, given the more immediate problems. She'd convinced herself that her mother's birth registration would be in the old format, but now wondered where to look next.

Dharma didn't log on to the internet for a couple of days. Her access wasn't unlimited, she'd taken a long lunch, and she was required to make up the time before the end of the week. She would begin again on Monday.

Six

Concord Penn glanced at Blythe as he sat at his station. She looked odd, but he couldn't work out why, except he was concerned that she might be sick. He'd been alone in the cubicle with her for more than a week, and they hadn't spoken in all that time. He missed Joy's company, even though he couldn't stand her. At least his responses to her tended to be emotional, even if those emotions were generally negative. He was merely indifferent to Blythe.

Blythe smelled the sweet hazelnut in Con's coffee. It brought her at least halfway back to reality. She cleared her private connection screen with a keystroke, and the usual invoice template popped up in front of her.

Con had come back to the cubicle a few minutes before she'd expected him, so Blythe sat quietly, while she settled her mind.

Con was looking over at her again.

"You look pale," he said.

"No!" said Blyth, surprised. She knew she wasn't sick, but she dreaded anyone else thinking she might be. It could set a whole system of protocols into action that she didn't need and couldn't cope with. Blythe's cheeks reddened, but the warm yellow of her skin tone remained pale. She looked drained. She tried a small smile on her co-worker.

Con backed his chair a little further from her, turning it on its wheels so that they were facing each other, about two metres apart. He peered at her. She really didn't want the attention, but she knew she had to answer for herself.

"Are you ill?" asked Con.

"No! It's just that I had a bit of a shock."

"What sort of a shock?"

"The shocking kind," said Blythe, her pallor gone, her face returning to its warmer shade. She smiled more broadly.

Nik Abnett

"Well, you don't look sick now," said Con, still peering at her. "And you're funny."

"All this time, and you hadn't worked that out?" asked Blythe.

"You don't talk much."

"Joy talks enough for all of us. Although, you seem to enjoy that."

"It's contact."

"Not any contact I'd want to be on the receiving end of," said Blythe. "I don't know how you put up with it."

"I don't know how you sit there, silent, when she's mouthing off about you," said Con.

"Touché."

They didn't speak for a moment.

"Are we actually having a conversation?" asked Blythe.

"Only if you tell me why you were pale," said Con, "what kind of shocking shock you suffered."

"Trust me, there was no suffering involved."

"So, tell me," said Con.

"Sorry," said Blythe. "Can't. Time to get back to work."

"I'll find out, one way or the other, so you might as well just tell me now."

Blythe had begun keying-in and checking the details on the latest of thousands of invoices that she'd processed. She said nothing, but turned to face Con, and smiled again.

"Okay, you win," he said, rolling his chair back to his station. "For now."

Seven

Verity was surprised that the queue wasn't longer.

"There are only a dozen people in front of us," she said, as she and Sage joined the line waiting for the campus infirmary to open.

"Everyone's gone," said Sage. "At least everyone who isn't already sick, who's got somewhere else to go."

"Well, now we have somewhere else to go," said Verity, smiling, and reaching for his hand.

Sage took it, and squeezed.

"Are you sure your dad's okay with this?" he asked.

"I told you," said Verity. "It was his idea."

"Yeah, but he only invited me so that you'd go home."

"Pa loves you," said Verity.

"'Pa' hardly knows me," said Sage.

"I love you, so he'll love you."

"That has not always been my experience with girlfriends' fathers," said Sage.

"And here I was thinking that I was the only one."

"You are," said Sage, dropping a quick kiss on her lips.

"Don't let anyone see you do that again," said Verity, smiling broadly. "It's not allowed, and, besides, you could give me this horrible thing."

"I was checking the net today. They've got to find a better name for it than 'TRRNT/41/pan-virus'."

"Some clever nutter on the internet will come up with something."

"Or some witty speech writer for the Prime Minister."

"Whoever we get to replace this one," said Verity. "He was diagnosed and quarantined overnight. Miserable ancient bastard isn't going to survive, is he?"

"Jeez, I didn't know," said Sage.

"Do you care?"

"He's a person. You've got to care."

25

"I think you're stretching the definition of 'person', right there," said Verity. "Pa didn't vote for him the first time, and none of us voted for him the second time."

"No," said Sage. "How long do you think this is going to take?"

"Nice way to change the subject. She looked along the line, and checked her watch, just as the doors to the infirmary were opening.

"I don't know," she said. "Couple of hours, maybe."

Two hours later there were still two people ahead of them in the queue, but at least they were inside the building. They'd had to strip, and go through a shower that smelled of something that reminded Verity of a nasty mixture of strong vinegar and bad eggs. Once out of the shower, they'd been given paper suits, face masks and shower caps. Verity had struggled to pile her hair on top of her head and tuck it all under the disposable cap. The men had all been required to shave, too. It didn't look good on the large, flabby man, sitting three chairs away on the other side of the waiting room, who'd stood in the queue, sporting an impressively dense beard. He hadn't been able to fasten the closures on his suit, either: One size didn't fit all. Verity decided not to look at him, but was still relieved when he stood up and disappeared behind one of the four doors that led off the waiting room.

"You go first," said Sage. "There's no point me getting checked out if you don't pass."

"Pa would still have you," said Verity.

"Maybe he would, but he'd hate me for ever, and forever is a long time to hide hatred."

"Okay. I'll go in first."

Another half-hour passed before it was Verity's turn.

She'd watched a dozen people go through those doors ahead of her, and none of them had come back. She wasn't sure whether they were all being quarantined, whether their time was up, or whether they were simply leaving by a different exit, so they didn't have to walk back past the rest of the people waiting for their checks. Either way, she hated leaving Sage. Worse still, they'd been told not to touch anyone once they'd gone through the shower, so she couldn't even hold his hand while they waited, and she couldn't kiss him when 'next' was called. She wanted, very badly to kiss him.

"See you on the other side, V," he said as she stood. "Love ya."

He was trying to keep things casual, but Verity was scared, and she knew that Sage was too.

She smiled down at him, his face tilted up, haloed by the strange shower cap.

"See you on the other side, pardner," she said, in a hinky American accent

As she walked towards the door, she wondered why she'd done that. To break the tension she supposed. It felt weird. How do you break that kind of tension?

The tests were not altogether pleasant, but almost the worst of it was being confronted by two medics in hazmat suits. She'd seen them on the TV, of course, and on the internet, but they were really weird up close, and Verity hadn't realised how strange the voices would be, filtered through the suit's headgear.

An instrument table had been set up with a kit on it, shrink-wrapped and foil-backed. Once she was naked again, the kit was opened. Swabs were taken from all over her body. A broad spatula was first passed over large areas of her skin. It was placed in a large tube so that the paddle was inserted into a liquid. The liquid changed colour.

Verity didn't know what that meant. She didn't know if the swab was positive or negative.

Small swabs followed. The mouth swab wasn't so bad, but the nasal swab was pushed deep into her sinuses, and made her gasp. It wasn't much fun having several hairs pulled out of her scalp, either. Then, more swabs were passed across her armpits and groin, and into her anus and vagina, and all while she was standing in the middle of the sterile room on a square of thick blue paper, which felt scrunchy, so clearly had a foil backing.

All the swabs were dropped into tubes of liquid, and they all changed colour. They all turned the same shade of acid yellow.

Verity had taken precautions from the beginning, mostly because her father had insisted on it. Pa was a pharmacist, so there was no reason to question his judgement. If anyone knew anything about any of this, it must surely be her father. She hadn't shown any symptoms, either.

Of course, Pa had wanted her to isolate herself entirely. Verity had decided on day one that she wouldn't and couldn't do that. Her roommate had left on the day the story had broken in the press, but that was weeks ago. She'd always been nervy, and took medication for anxiety, so Verity wasn't surprised to see her go. In fact, she hadn't had a chance to see her go or say goodbye to her. When Verity had returned home the afternoon of the Prime Minister's announcement, the flat had simply been stripped of everything that didn't belong to her, and the girl was gone. The note on the wipe-board was brief and to the point: 'Can't stay. Might be back next term. K'.

Verity didn't dislike her, but they weren't close. The big advantage of her roommate leaving was that she and Sage could go into isolation together.

"Do you really want to?" Sage had asked when she'd phoned him. "Do you really think we need to?"

"That's not the point, Sage," said Verity. "Three or four weeks in our own little love nest might be fun."

"Now you're talking."

Sage moved into Verity's flat late on the same day her roommate had left. He brought one backpack with a change of clothes and study materials, and several bags of food. Sage lived off porridge, baked beans and ramen noodles, and he hated to shop, so he had enough to last them for weeks. Whatever happened, they wouldn't starve.

"You're so clever," said Verity. "Who knew that eating badly could be a good thing?"

"What are you talking about?" Sage asked, smiling. "We've got all the food groups covered: Breakfast, lunch and dinner."

And that's how it had been. They'd studied, separately, one in each of the tiny single bedrooms, and they'd shared the living room with its pull-out sofa. Sage even managed to make porridge taste good without milk.

They'd left everything behind when they'd gone to the infirmary. All they had were the clothes on their backs, their phones, their ids and debit cards, and some small items of jewellery, including Verity's watch. It had all been taken away for fumigation while they had their checks.

One of the medics in a hazmat suit took several minutes filling out a form on a steel clipboard. She finished with an odd flourish, obviously a signature.

Suddenly, Verity was sweating. She felt a bead on her forehead, and a drip from her armpit. This was it. It felt like some kind of terrible judgement day.

The medic divided up the form, which Verity assumed to be in triplicate, dropped one into a ziplock folder and sealed it, dropped one into a slot in the wall, slid one into a covered tray under the metal table, and finally handed a copy to Verity.

Not triplicate, quadruplicate, Verity thought as she took her copy. She studied it, but didn't have a clue what all the numbers and tick-boxes signified. She looked at the medic.

The medic smiled, and gave Verity a thumbs up.

"Acid yellow just became my favourite colour," said Verity. "Thank you... Thank you so much."

She wanted to hug the medic, as she felt herself tear up.

"You're welcome," said the medic. "You're one of the very lucky few, so look after yourself. Now, off you go."

"Really, thank you." Verity looked around for her clothes, since she was still naked and the paper suit had disappeared.

"Through there," said the medic, pointing to a door on the left. There were two other doors, besides the one that Verity had entered by, and they were identical. It was all very anonymous. "By the way, I'd also recommend you cut your hair,"

"Yes. I'm guessing going to the hairdresser's is out of the question?" She was beaming, but the medic didn't respond.

"Here," she said, handing Verity a pair of scissors that were in the kit, along with all the swabs and tubes.

"Now?" asked Verity.

"Why not?" said the medic. "We can incinerate it for you. Best practice."

Verity hesitated, looking at the scissors. She wondered why they were in the kit, if it wasn't for cutting hair. She didn't know where to start.

"Just hack everything off, up to your chin for now," said the medic. "You can sort out the rest when you get to where you're going… Home to your parents, I presume."

"Yes," said Verity, the full weight of realisation falling on her all at once. "I'm going home."

She cut her hair off, parting it down the back, and shearing through half of it at a time. The medic stepped on the pedal of a medical waste bin next to the instrument table and Verity dropped the hair in. Then she took hold of the other half of her hair, and repeated the process.

"Good job," said the medic.

"Thank you," Verity said, through tears. It wasn't the loss of her hair but the thought that soon she would be home with her parents and with Sage, and then she'd know for sure that they'd all live through this. She hadn't realised how much pressure she'd felt over the past few weeks, cooped up in the tiny flat. At first it had been fun, but for the last week or so there had been nothing new to study on the boards from her professors and tutors. The food had got boring a while ago, and they'd begun to ration it over the past fortnight.

The only good thing about their isolation was that Verity and Sage had become a team and a great comfort for one another.

Verity hadn't realised how emotional the check-up would be, but now she was certified to travel and had the form to prove it; and she had the e-tickets on her phone to get on the next train home. She felt overwhelmed.

Verity thanked the medic again, even going so far as to blow her a kiss, before going through the door into the tiny room, to dress in her freshly fumigated plastic-wrapped clothes, and pick up her freshly fumigated plastic-wrapped belongings. There was a laminated instruction card, with time and transport details, presumably also fumigated. She checked the time. Fifteen minutes before she had to leave the infirmary. She also noticed that, while the room was empty of furniture, there was a clock on the wall. Clearly, time was of the essence.

Verity thought about that blown kiss, and the hinky accent she'd used when she'd said goodbye to Sage. She thought about the crying and the smiling she'd done in front of the medic, and the range of emotions she'd experienced in so short a time. This stuff changed people. It made her feel differently, think differently, even act differently. She guessed it was the same for everyone: they were all reacting in odd ways to their new situations.

None of it really mattered, because today was a good day. She had the all-clear, and she could go home. All she had to do was wait for Sage.

When her fifteen minutes were up, Verity hesitated for a moment, before pushing the handle on the fire exit door. It swung closed behind her. A limo had pulled up, its engine running. Verity knew that the car was for her, but was surprised that it was a limo rather than an ordinary taxi. Then it dawned on her that it was a limo because of the screen. The driver was separated from the passenger cabin by a privacy screen. He glanced at her, and she could see the precautions he'd taken. He was wearing one of the shower caps, and a face mask, and his uniform appeared to be one of the same paper suits that she'd worn in the infirmary.

Clearly, no one was taking any chances.

Verity hesitated, reluctant to leave without Sage. She didn't have to wait for long.

She heard the clunk of a fire door opening to her right, and she turned. Sage stepped through the door, looking pale and anxious. He hadn't seen her yet.

"Sage!" said Verity, surprised by the pitch and volume of her voice.

Sage didn't care that Verity's voice was too high and too loud, he was simply thrilled to see her; more thrilled than he had thought possible, despite his anxiety in exiting the infirmary. He'd barely had time to dress before he had to be out of the building, in time for his transport, according to the clock on the wall of the little room.

He walked towards Verity and stopped short.

"Your hair!"

"It's better this way, and Mum can help me tidy it up when we get home."

"No, I like it." He hesitated. "Should we touch?"

"I don't know. I want to."

"Me too," said Sage. "It's all been a bit crazy, though, hasn't it?"

"Crazy?" asked Verity. "More like scary as hell."

They both smiled.

"Glad I'm not the only one feeling it," said Sage.

"You're definitely not the only one."

Sage became aware that the limo driver was watching them.

"Better get in. Don't want to miss our chance, and that guy looks antsy."

"How can you tell behind that mask?"

"Oh," said Sage. "I can tell."

They got into the back of the limo, one through each passenger door. The inside was big enough to seat six, with three seats facing each other. They both chose the middle seats, opposite each other.

As soon as they'd closed the doors, the driver pulled the limousine away on the first leg of their journey.

"Just us," said Sage.

"Looks like."

"We could have caught it right there in that queue."

"But we didn't," said Verity. "And we don't know we're the only ones. Some of the others might have left an hour or more ago."

"I hope so."

"Me too," said Verity, "even though I've got everything… every*one* I need, right here."

They expected a short drive to the station, especially as there was very little traffic on the roads, but they were in the limousine for close to an hour, taking them three stops further down the track.

Sage checked his phone.

"It's fine," he said, as he could see Verity's growing anxiety. "They've closed a lot of the smaller stations, and they're monitoring passengers through mainline stations. The trains are still running. It's all a precaution."

"According to who?" Verity asked.

"According to the government."

"We still have one of those?"

"It looks like it, and I suspect there'll be a whole lot more government intervention before this thing's over."

"It was supposed to be over by now," said Verity.

"Things change. I sometimes wonder if anyone really knows anything."

"We know we're going home. At least, we know we're going home."

They encountered more hazmat-suited workers on their journey, and had to show their certificates before getting on the train. Even so, they were blasted with hand-held air jets that had the same funky smell as the showers in the infirmary.

They were allowed to sit together on the train, but there were only three other people in the carriage, and their seats were assigned, so that they wouldn't come into contact with each other. The same awful smell permeated the inside of the train. There was no access to a bathroom.

It took a couple of hours to get to St Pancras, and there was no one to meet them there: No buses, no taxis, and the underground was closed.

"There's nobody around," said Sage.

"Hardly anybody," Verity agreed, as she gestured towards a man walking around a street corner a hundred metres away.

"Wasn't he on the train with us?" asked Sage.

"I think he was. Apparently he knows where he's going, but I thought there was going to be a pick-up, so we could get home." She looked at her travel documentation.

"I'll check my phone," said Sage.

Verity waited as Sage scrolled for information.

"There's no public transport in London, apart from the mainline trains, and travellers have to carry current certificates," he finally told her. "The car services were suspended as of about an hour ago."

"So, what do we do?" She didn't wait for an answer. "I'm gonna call Pa."

"Not a bad first move. I don't expect he'll be able to do much, though. It's not as if he can drive up and get us."

"Pa," said Verity. "We're in London, outside St Pancras station." She paused for a moment while her father said something.

"Yeah, I know," she said. "How do we get home?"

She paused again for several seconds, listening. "Thanks, Pa," she finally said. "Love you too."

"What did he say?" asked Sage.

"It's all fine," she said, bending at the waist, her hands on her thighs, knees bent, as she took a breath and steadied herself.

"You don't look fine."

"Just panicked for a minute. Really, I'm Okay."

Verity stood up, and smiled at Sage. "It's nothing. We've just got a bit of a walk ahead of us. It'll be fun; we'll see some sites."

"A bit of a walk?" Sage asked.

"Pa reckons it's nine miles. It's basically a straight line from here to Catford, on the A2."

"Nine miles. We can walk nine miles."

"Of course we can."

"At four miles an hour, it'll only take a couple of hours or so."

"Let's try for three hours, and be happy with four," said Verity. "I'm just glad I put my sneakers on this morning."

"Shall we?" asked Sage, offering Verity his hand.

She took it, and they looked around to get their bearings before heading south.

Eight

"Don't you usually go out for lunch about now, Concord?" Blythe asked.

She'd been waiting for him to leave so that she could have the cubicle to herself for forty minutes, and have some more contact with Dharma.

"Not today," said Con. "And I rather like that you call me Concord. I've never been a big fan of the abbreviation; makes me feel like a villain."

"Aren't you?" asked Blythe.

"Nope."

"But you're not going to lunch?"

"I'm afraid you might have another shocking shock while I'm gone, and I'd feel horribly responsible, so I thought I'd stay, and keep you company."

"I'd rather be alone," said Blythe.

"Which only worries me more. It's decided, I'm staying here to make sure you don't faint or swoon or something."

"Swoon?" said Blythe, smiling.

"So, I like nineteenth century novels," said Con. "What of it?"

"I might be funny, but you're just plain weird."

"You're not the first person to tell me that."

"You seem different."

"From what?"

"I don't know, but I see the way you are with Joy, and it doesn't make me like you."

"It doesn't make me like me, either," said Con, "but I haven't had a peep out of you in... how many years? I admit it, I'm one of those people for whom any company is better than no company, even if it means listening to Joy moaning for hours at a time."

"Then I feel sorry for you," said Blythe.

"Don't. It might have taken me a while to realise it, but now that I see how funny and mysterious you are, you've got my interest."

35

"Well, now I feel sorry for Joy," said Blythe, smiling. "And a little bit sorry for myself. You're a user Concord Penn."

"And now my heart is broken," said Con, clutching at his chest in dramatic fashion. "But can we stop messing about, now, and get on with whatever it is you're secretly getting on with."

Blythe had felt alone in the cubicle since she'd arrived, and it'd been far too long. She liked that Con thought her funny. She *was* funny. She hardly had anyone, except for her frightful mother, at least not until she got to know Dharma better. Con was in the cubicle with her and, okay, he was nosy, but he was also amusing, warmer than she expected, and nicer than she had ever thought possible.

"Okay," she said, "I'll send you what I got yesterday, and you can read it, but you can also keep your comments to yourself."

"Done!" said Con, rolling his chair back up to his station, and opening the document she'd uploaded to him.

Five minutes later, Blythe asked, over her shoulder, "You sure you don't want to get out for your lunch? You've still got half an hour."

"Shh, I'm reading."

Blythe turned back to her own screen, and the private connection she'd opened with Dharma. Overnight, or, at least since she'd closed the private connection the previous day, more stuff had dropped into her box, much more. Dharma had gathered a massive amount of information. There were data sheets with charts and names, dates and places, and there were lots of text documents, mostly in the form of stream of consciousness. Dharma had obviously been talking fast when she'd opened the connection.

"Do you believe this stuff?" asked Con, several minutes later. "I mean, how can this Dharma person possibly think she's related to you?"

"What part of 'keep your comments to yourself' did you not understand?" asked Blythe.

"You can't just drop this on me, and not talk about it. It's pretty huge."

"It is, isn't it?" said Blythe, smiling.

"Seriously," said Con, "how could anyone possibly find out this kind of stuff?"

"That's the first thing I asked her. She's a data analyst, working for W.W. and she's ninetieth percentile. So, I guess, that's how."

"All that proves is that she wanted to stay home with her mother for as long as possible."

"Maybe," said Blythe, "but plenty of people manage that without getting her level of education."

"But you only know what she's telling you. There's no way to verify this stuff. Aren't you suspicious?"

"What's to be suspicious about?"

"Well, for a start," said Con. "She's a total stranger."

"Aren't we all?"

"You and me aren't strangers."

"All I know about you is that you like your coffee too sweet and too nutty," said Blythe. "It's not a whole lot, is it?"

Con stopped reading the data, and turned his chair to face her. The sound of the moving casters made Blythe look around.

"I know even less about you," said Con. "Except that you're beautiful and funny, and too quiet. It's still more than we know about her."

"Not now," said Blythe. She didn't know Con well enough for him to get personal, and it made her uncomfortable.

"We could get to know each other," said Con.

Blythe turned her chair to face him.

"Look Con," she said. "We've been sitting in this cubicle for three years, and barely spoken a dozen words, what makes you think I want to get to know you now?"

Con looked a little crestfallen.

"My first priority is Dharma. She's taken some time and effort, not to mention connection power, to find me and reach out to me. What did you ever do?"

"You're right," said Con.

"It might be better if you took your lunch break," said Blythe. "You've still got time to get a cup of coffee, at least."

"Right." Con cleared his screen, pulled on a sweater, and left the cubicle.

Blythe sighed, and turned back to her screen. Dharma's uploads were comprehensive but there was a lot of data. It had been well organised, and Dharma had made notes so that Blythe could navigate the material, but it was still a huge amount, and, if true, it was an awful lot to take in.

"Dharma Tuke," said Blythe, closing her eyes for a moment, "and Blythe Dole." The names felt good to her, side-by-side in her head. They sounded good out loud, too.

Time was almost up, so Blythe cleared her connection, and a new invoice for Anley Corp filled her screen. She stood up, stretched, and looked out through the acrylic wall. The floor was quiet.

The door opened behind her as Con entered the cubicle. She didn't turn around.

"Peace offering," he said. "I guess you like yours without hazelnut, but I took a punt on the milk. You're right, I never did make an effort with you."

Blythe turned around, and took the coffee that Con held out to her.

"Thank you."

"We could be friends," said Con, sitting at his station, ready to get back to work. "Maybe?"

"Maybe."

It was true that he hadn't ever taken an interest in her, but that worked both ways. She'd been the last into the cubicle, so Joy and Con already knew each other. She could have been more forthcoming when she'd first arrived.

Blythe had always struggled with social connections. She liked to have people physically close, partly because her mother had always been such a huge presence in her life. It wasn't her choice, and her mother was demanding of her shy daughter. Nevertheless, Blythe knew that she could make more of an effort, especially with her co-workers.

Her excitement over her new connection with Dharma was palpable. She had thought about little else for the past couple of days. She had only three days remaining to cement the relationship, three forty minute sessions. She hoped it would be enough.

She hoped that Dharma would find her as interesting as she found Dharma. She wasn't sure that was possible. Tomorrow, she'd stop looking at data, and spend those forty minutes keying in some information about herself. She'd send Dharma a proper introductory e-mail.

Blythe and Concord didn't speak for the next couple of hours. They simply worked at their computer stations, as usual. Only the sounds of the circulating air, and fingers on keyboards broke the silence.

"The coffee was good," Blythe said, when a new invoice appeared in front of her for the umpteenth time. She didn't turn to look at Con, speaking to the screen. "Just how I like it."

"I'll remember that," said Con.

It was a beginning.

Nine

Dharma sat at home all weekend, taking notes and making plans for her search.

Most weekends she still jogged; she felt it kept her sane while she grieved the loss of her mother. She never took the long, circuitous route back to where her mother had lived. She changed routes often, but always made circuits, so that she didn't need to fill in forms for travelling outside the two square miles of her own district. BRd1 was old, built almost entirely before the Deluge, and the streets were tightly packed and at odd angles. If she'd been able to jog to her mother's as the crow flies, it would be a little less than two miles, but following the streets, tacking this way and that, it ended up being three miles.

Like everyone else, Dharma took the most direct routes from home to work, and anywhere else she had to visit: the medical centre for her check-ups, and the market for supplies on her allotted days. There were streets, even within her two-square-mile world, that she had never been down before, buildings she had never seen, and faces, too. Some of those faces looked back at her with suspicion, many crossed the street or walked into a building if she came within ten metres of them. During one jog, she had come very close to a sallow-skinned man with a large nose, as she turned a corner. They had both put up their hands, and Dharma had scheduled a check-up for the following day. She assumed that the man had too, if the horror on his face was any indication.

Changing her route regularly, to get her three mile jog, Dharma began to think there were a great many more things to see and do, and more people to know, than she had ever considered before. She reminded herself that they were not her blood. She reminded herself that she worked alone from choice.

Since she was alone in her apartment and no longer pursuing an education, Dharma's computer access was limited to personal data, including photos, and entertainment streaming. She could read a book or watch shows and movies. She'd always been a keen reader, but had never bothered with visual art forms much. Once in a while she'd watch the latest movie, but since the Deluge, they were all animated or CGI. Her mother had liked watching the old archived stuff, acted by real people. The trouble was they were antiquated, and it was difficult to watch people crowded together or touching each other without the protocols. As a child, she'd once seen a movie where two people had touched their mouths together. It had made her cry with fear, but her mother had reassured her that it was called kissing, and that people had done it for hundreds of years, maybe thousands.

"That doesn't make it right," Dharma had said, and her mother had turned off the screen so that her daughter could read out-loud to her instead. She was a good reader, even at eight years old.

Dharma went to work as normal the following Monday, determined to broaden her search efficiently. She wasn't allowed to bring anything to work, nobody was, but she retained data easily, especially once she'd written it down, and she could reproduce the notes she'd made over the weekend without a second's thought or hesitation.

At one o'clock, Dharma switched from the W.W. intranet connection to her internet access. Her first search was for a list of 'boroughs of London'. She looked at the thirty or so names in dismay. This could be a long search.

Summoning a map, she quickly identified the London Borough of Bromley by its shape. It sat squarely in the lower right quadrant. If her mother had been right when she'd called BRd1 'Bromley', then this section of the map represented home.

Dharma needed to broaden her search. The town of Bromley was in the top left quadrant of the borough map, so she looked first at the boroughs closest to the red boundary line: Croydon to the west and Lewisham to the north.

Dharma called up a map of the London Borough of Croydon, since it was next alphabetically.

She pulled up the birth registry.

"Constance Tuke," she said, "25th October 2042. Croydon."

+Data not found+

"Correction: Addington."

+Data not found+

"Correction: Addiscombe."

+Data not found+

Dharma continued through all the grey patches on the green map, starting with the largest. The answer always came back the same.

She began to wonder how long this was going to take her, and, if she succeeded, how long it would then take her to find any details about her grandmother. And, even if it was possible to find her grandmother, where would she go from there?

"I'm a data analyst," she said to the screen. "This isn't going to beat me."

The screen blinked.

+Data not recognised+

+Communication?+

"Negative," said Dharma. "Constance Tuke, 25th October, 2042. Thornton Heath."

+Data not found+

When Dharma went back to work an hour later, her job seemed infinitely easier than this search had become. She'd drawn blank after blank, and she'd only just managed to exhaust the place names in the borough of Croydon before her time was up. She hadn't started on Lewisham yet, and what if that didn't give her a result? There were more than thirty boroughs in London alone. What if her mother had been born even further afield?

Surely that wasn't possible.

"Nobody moves," said Dharma, as she paced in her cubicle, thinking more about her search than about her job. "Nobody moved during the Deluge. People were assigned housing in the New Wave. She can't be far away. She's got to be here, somewhere."

A data box was glowing on the screen as Dharma glanced at it.

+Data discontinued+

She hadn't offered a VR command or made a keystroke in more than five minutes. She must get back to work.

"Download data R478/J field F."

The data box disappeared, and Dharma concentrated on her job for the rest of the afternoon. This thing could wait until tomorrow, or the day after that, or next week, next month, or even next year, if necessary.

Dharma was used to working on projects over extended periods of time. It was her job. She could treat her personal project like a job, too. It meant that she could only spend five computer hours a week on this, but, if she worked fast enough, and organised the data efficiently, analysing it would be straightforward.

The records were all in the public domain, all she had to do was verify and cross reference them once she'd found them. It was nothing.

Dharma pushed back her lunch break to two o'clock on Tuesday. The anticipation was easier to deal with than the disappointment, and, this way, her working afternoon would be shortened.

At precisely two o'clock, Dharma switched to the internet, and began her search through the place names in the London Borough of Lewisham.

"Constance Tuke, 25th October 2042. Lewisham," she said.

+Data not found+

"Constance Tuke, 25th October 2042. Catford."

There was no data box.

Dharma held her breath, and stared intently at the screen. A form appeared on it with her mother's name, and date and place of birth. So far, so good.

Down the right hand side of the screen there was an insert with further options. Dharma read one of them out, "View full certificate," she said.

Another data box.

+Payment required+

"Checkout." She had no idea what charge would be made for viewing the certificate. She was on a decent wage, but much of her pay cheque was allocated for her accommodation and services, and she'd chosen a reasonably high tariff, valuing comfort at home above other things. If the charges were significant, she might have to make an adjustment to her service tariff to allow her to spend money on finding a living, genetic relation.

+Four tix+

Dharma smiled. It was nothing. She could call up dozens of certificates, if she had to, before the cost would make a dent in her standard of living.

She held her id card up to the scanner, and a moment later the certificate was displayed on the screen.

Dharma studied it long and hard. She ignored the geographical data along the top, except to confirm that the birth had been registered in Catford. Date of birth matched her mother's birthday and place of birth was given as 131, Engleheart Road, Catford, SE6, in accordance with the old form of address. It made sense that, during the Deluge, a birth would take place at home rather than a hospital, as seemed the norm pre-Deluge. As yet, she saw no reason to distrust this certificate.

She zoomed in and scrolled right, revealing two more columns. The first listed the father's name as 'Sage Endeavour Tuke', which settled it. She already knew that her grandfather had been called Sage Tuke."

She felt a sense of disconnect, as if the certificate related to events from hundreds of years ago. Dharma knew that she had met her grandmother, and if this was her grandfather she had a blood bond to him, too. It felt strange. She didn't believe in ghosts, even in the stories that she read, but if there was ever a time for ghosts it was during the Deluge.

Dharma took a deep breath, and let it go slowly, before looking at the next column; it should show her grandmother's name, and it did. 'Verity Cornelia Tuke' was arranged over three lines of text.

Underneath her grandmother's name were the words, 'formerly Mott.'

Was Dharma's grandmother Verity Mott?

"Scroll down," she said.

There were three more lines of text that read, 'of 131 Engleheart Road, Catford'.

Verity Mott, who was most likely Dharma's grandmother, had given birth at home.

The next column indicated that the father of the baby was not employed. That tallied with her mother's stories about her grandparents being students when they met. Dharma didn't know whether either of her grandparents had completed their educations, but she did know that the old style of educational institutions, before the Deluge, had been shut down for the duration of the crisis, and, during the New Wave, home education had been developed and introduced.

Dharma also knew that millions had lost their jobs during the Deluge. No unnecessary work was done for eighteen months, and much of the necessary work was already being done by machines and computers by the start of the twenty-first century.

The next column surprised Dharma. The informant of the birth had been a man called Pax Mott, described as 'grandfather', and resident at the same address as Sage and Verity. Dharma looked at the date of registration, almost exactly six weeks after the birth, on Friday 5th of December 2042.

Dharma had an analytical mind, and it all made sense to her. The Deluge was coming to an end by the beginning of 2043. There were no new cases in December of 2042, so perhaps the isolation rules were beginning to be relaxed. Nevertheless, a father would, naturally be careful of his child and grandchild, and an older man would be more willing to risk his life in place of a young one. Anyone would have the sense to wait for as long as possible before going out into the world to perform any task. Her mother's grandfather had waited for five weeks and six days, and then he had left his home, his daughter and his grand-daughter, and travelled to that office, probably on foot, to register the birth of the child, presumably as late as legislation allowed.

Dharma admired him hugely for it. She wondered what he had done for work, and who he had been, other than a clearly doting father.

She wanted this to be her family. She was only surprised that four people could be living together in a single dwelling. That could never happen now.

"Upload to home stream," said Dharma. "Photo storage."

It was a risk, and she knew it, but Dharma wanted more time to examine the document, to consider the implications. She didn't *have* more time at work, so she would do it at home. W.W. was free to check uploads between office and domestic locations, but Dharma suspected the checks were randomised and infrequent. W.W. wouldn't waste its computing power on such trivial things.

If the upload was checked, she'd simply claim an academic interest in family history and genealogy. It was an unusual hobby, one she'd never heard of anyone pursuing, but the records were in the public domain, so someone was looking at them, probably lots of someones.

Ten

"Weird, isn't it?" said Sage, less than an hour into their long walk to Verity's family home.

"The last time I was in London it was heaving," said Verity. "There were cars and buses everywhere, and people... Millions of people!"

"Well, they're all behind closed doors, now."

"You can actually hear the pigeons," said Verity. "I guess this thing doesn't kill them."

"Guess not. Or, maybe, it just hasn't got to them yet. People have been having their pets euthanized."

"I was reading about that on the net, the other day. There's speculation that it's not because of the thing. They reckon it's because of food shortages."

"Oh. That's horrible."

"Yes, but this isn't." Verity stepped off the pavement and walked into the middle of the road. She stood on the white line, put her arms out to either side of her body, and began to walk the line as if she was doing a sobriety test, or walking a tightrope.

"It'll take forever to walk to Catford like that," said Sage, but at least he was smiling now.

Verity had coped better than Sage with the news that was constantly being uploaded to the net. Most of it wasn't news at all. Most of it was speculation, probably from the uninformed, and almost always from the terrified. Others seemed to take pleasure in this horrible crisis. She wished she hadn't mentioned that people were killing their pets so they didn't have to feed them. It was gruesome, and it probably wasn't even true.

She felt much more upbeat since they'd found an alley between two rows of houses, where they could duck in for a pee. They'd taken it in turns to stand at the end of the alley and keep watch. They'd seen nobody.

"Let's skip for a bit," said Verity.

"Seriously, V?"

"Race you to the end of the street," said Verity, taking off at a quick jog, before Sage knew what was happening.

It didn't stop him beating her.

"How are you so quick on your feet when your diet is so damned awful?" asked Verity, coming up beside him, a little out of breath.

"You don't know the half of it. Besides, think of all those good carbs I get: Oats, legumes... Nothing wrong with them."

"Left or right?" asked Verity.

Sage pointed over his shoulder at the corner street sign, where the A2 south was clearly posted.

"No need to check the phone again," he said. "How's your battery, mine's getting pretty low."

"I'm still good. I charged mine before we left the flat."

"I knew there was a reason I loved you," said Sage.

"Clear off!" said a voice from somewhere above them, and on the other side of the road. "You shouldn't be fooling about outside, you could be contagious."

Sage pulled his travel certificate out of his pocket, and waved it in the direction of the voice. He could see that someone in a first floor flat, over a shop, had cracked a window a fraction, but he couldn't see who was inside.

"We've got travel clearance, see?" said Sage.

"I don't care what you've got!" said the voice. "I just don't want you to give it to me."

"Of course, sir," said Sage. "We've got a long walk, and my girlfriend needs a rest."

"I told you to fuck off!" said the voice, and the window closed before Sage could say anything else.

"Millions behind closed doors," said Verity. "Come on. The sooner we get home the better."

For the next two hours, Verity and Sage saw no one. They heard a dog barking occasionally, which reassured Sage that people were, after all, decent; and two or three times they heard the blurred words of people shouting at each other from behind closed doors.

"It's not for everyone is it?" asked Sage.

"What isn't for everyone?"

"Being cooped up at home with only family for company. People are arguing... Even screaming at each other... Makes you wonder."

"Well obviously it makes you wonder, but what exactly are you wondering about?"

"Whether this is a good idea," said Sage.

"We're going home," said Verity. "Everyone argues once in a while. My parents, not so much, but, you know, sometimes."

"It's going to be stressful, though isn't it? All of us in one house, and them not really knowing me."

"It'll be fine," said Verity, taking Sage's hand as he slowed his pace.

"I don't know. We were doing okay on our own, and this feels pretty final. Once we're there, we won't be going anywhere... And who knows how long this thing's going to last?"

"Then they'll have time to get to know and love you, like I do."

"I don't know," said Sage, again.

"Well, you don't need to know. Because *I* know. I know that we had no choice but to leave campus. I know that we've taken a long and difficult journey, and it isn't over yet. I know there's no going back. And I know that every hotel, guesthouse, B-and-B, motel... whatever... is closed for business. So, unless you want to wander off into the woods and become some kind of hermit, we're committed."

"I'd make a good hermit."

Verity stopped in her tracks, and laughed.

"What? What's so funny?"

"Well, apart from the fact that you've only got the clothes on your back, a practically dead phone, your id, and a travel certificate, nothing about you becoming a hermit is funny. I'm guessing you can build a shelter, find a clean water supply, and hunt and forage for food with the best of them."

"So you could do better, could you?"

"I don't need to do better," said Verity. "I've got a plan. You can join in if you like." She smiled at him, and took his hand.

"I guess we're going to your parents' place, then."

49

"Great plan," said Verity, mock-serious. "Wish I'd thought of it first."

They started walking again, through more streets of boarded up shops, and houses, the pigeons doing their thing, and occasional sounds coming from behind closed doors.

"You can't actually take credit for the plan," said Sage.

"I think I can."

"I'm pretty sure it was your dad's plan. I'm pretty sure you resisted it for weeks. In fact, getting on board with the plan was all a bit last minute for you, wasn't it, V?"

"When we arrive, Pa will tell you himself that he's always right."

They walked another mile or two, holding hands. Then, suddenly, Verity crossed the road, working up to a short run, and then a jump. The metal sign clanged as she hit it hard with her open palm. It read, 'Catford'.

"I told Pa I'd call when we got close. I know my way from here. We'll be home in fifteen minutes."

"That soon?" asked Sage.

"You've got fifteen minutes to sort out your head, and brace yourself for a warm welcome, so you'd better get it together."

"Hi, Pa, we're here." There was a short pause. "About fifteen minutes, we're standing under the Catford sign right now."

Sage waited while Verity listened to her father.

"Yes, Pa. I've got it... No, I don't need to repeat it back to you... Yes, I totally get it... Yep... See you soon. Love ya."

"They're ready for us," she said, after she'd hung up.

Eleven

"You could let me help you," said Con.

"Help me with what?" asked Blythe, over her shoulder as she completed her last invoice of the morning.

"It's time for lunch. You could let me help you with this Dharma thing."

"I was just going to write her a long e-mail, today."

"Even more reason, then," said Con. "I could use the time to check her data, if you like... Objectively."

"You don't think I'm objective?" asked Blythe, as she switched her screen to her private connections.

"There's a lot of text, that's all. I could just look at the data. I could see if there are any problems with the sequences. I could work out whether you might actually be related to this person, from the data she's provided."

"You want to sit and check data for me?" asked Blythe.

"I think maybe someone should. This doesn't happen, does it? People don't just invite you to make private connections for no reason. It's all a bit suspect..."

Con paused when he saw the look on Blythe's face.

"I know you think it's wonderful," he said. "If it was me, I'd be pretty pleased, too. I'm just saying, it couldn't hurt to check the data."

"I've looked at most of it. Besides, what makes you think you're qualified?"

"Nothing. I may not work for W.W. but I'm in the ninetieth percentile, too."

"Oh..."

There was a pause. Blythe had questions about Con that she wasn't sure she wanted to ask.

"Okay," said Con, eventually. "I'm going to pop down and get us both some coffee while you think about it... It couldn't hurt to have a fresh pair of eyes."

"I'll see you in five minutes," said Blythe. She just wanted to write to Dharma and get as much down in one e-mail as she had time for. She wanted to talk about herself and about her mum, and she wanted to ask questions, too. She wanted to know what Dharma looked and sounded like, what she did, and how and where she lived. She already felt something about this woman who had sought her out... This stranger.

Blythe took a deep breath, and uploaded the data files for Con to look at. She'd ask about his education one day, but maybe now wasn't the time. It couldn't hurt for him to take a look, especially since he was clearly qualified. They were just spread sheets, just data... It'd be fine, useful even.

She kept the text files to herself.

Con came back with two cups of coffee from the machine. He took off his sweater, and hung it on one of the door hooks.

"Oh," he said, on glancing at his screen.

"It's not that I trust you or anything. I'm just taking advantage of your qualifications, so don't get the idea that we're friends... yet."

"Of course not," said Con. "All in good time."

Although it stated quite clearly in her contract that Anley Corp would not monitor her private connections, Blythe knew that they would see anything that she transferred to Con's screen, and she wondered whether uploading the first long e-mail from Dharma had been a good idea. The data didn't matter, at least not so much, but the text files were pretty personal, even the first one. It was too late now, but she decided that she wouldn't do it again. He could see data uploads; it might even help her, but if she wanted to show him any of the text files, he'd have to read them from her screen.

Why was she thinking about that at all? There was no reason why she'd ever want to share anything personal with Con. He wasn't the guy she'd thought he was; he was better than that. She didn't know if they'd ever be friends, though. She didn't know if she'd ever really *had* a friend. Her mother had never encouraged it, and when faced with new people Blythe was always timid. Twenty years of relying entirely on her mother, who invariably spoke for her, and then ten years on her own with her mother's warnings constantly on her mind, had made Blythe incredibly cautious.

There was stuff to deal with, of course, but she always booked the same medic at the clinic. She'd developed the habit of booking her next appointment after seeing the medic, even though it would be three or four months away. It didn't matter, she wasn't going anywhere. She always used the same vendors at the market on her allocated days, and she always bought the same things. She'd even managed to get a spare canister for her bathroom wipe, though it was discouraged because of storage and use-by dates.

Blythe's life was one continuous routine, and that's how she liked it. Perhaps that was why she hadn't managed to speak to Con for the first three years. She wanted company, she wanted a friend, even; she just didn't know how to make one.

Now, Dharma wasn't just offering friendship she was offering kinship, and kinship apart from the maternal bond was practically unheard of since the Deluge.

Blythe's mother didn't talk about the forties, or the fifties. She didn't even talk about Blythe's childhood. She didn't care for the past, and the state could take care of the future; that's what she'd told Blythe, over and over again. She still said it, every time they talked. It was like a mantra, and there was no penetrating it.

Dharma didn't think like that.

Dharma had taken a long hard look at the past. She had looked so hard that she had found her own personal history, not just the stuff that Blythe had studied when she'd downloaded school. Her mother hadn't encouraged her there, either. Blythe had only taken the mandatory classes. When she'd shown an interest in anything else, her mother had nipped it in the bud. It was all useless, she'd said, Blythe would never need any of it in the real world.

Well, this *was* the real world. Dharma was real, and Blythe was sure that Dharma's research was real, too. Why else would the woman reach out to her? What possible motive could there be?

Blythe suddenly felt a little anxious.

"Anything?" she asked, over her shoulder.

"Nothing yet," said Con. "It all looks feasible, on the surface."

Blythe sighed and returned to her email. She read back what had already been typed and was shocked at how personal it all was. Stream of consciousness, just like Dharma's e-mails to her.

"Almost time to stop," said Con.

She couldn't believe that she'd been typing through their entire lunch break, and her coffee sat, untouched and barely lukewarm.

Blythe didn't think twice. She hit the send button. Whatever she'd been thinking, whatever she'd typed, Dharma could read it. It didn't matter that it was personal, and it didn't matter that her grammar and spelling, and that her rhythm and syntax might not be correct or elegant. It mattered that she connected.

This was the longest conversation of her life. The most she'd ever talked to anyone, and it mattered very much to Blythe.

Con and Blythe cleared their screens at almost the same moment. Con turned his chair.

"Hey?" he said.

Blythe picked up her coffee cup, and turned her chair to face him.

"I haven't been through everything yet," he said. "But I can't find any obvious anomalies... I'd like to be more sure, and I'd like to see the source material."

"It's not your job," said Blythe.

"Okay," said Con, putting up his hands and rolling his chair back.

"I didn't mean it like that," said Blythe, smiling slightly, and then taking a sip of her coffee.

"Isn't that cold?"

"You went to get it for me. The least I can do is drink it... And, no, not quite cold yet. Why are you doing this?" she continued.

"Do you know what I usually do during my lunch break?"

"How would I know that? I don't leave the cubicle for lunch."

"I walk around the block," said Con. "I alternate. One day, I walk around the block clock-wise, and the next anti-clock-wise. I'd really like to walk around with a cup of coffee, but that would feel strange. So I pick up a coffee before I come back in, so it goes through the wipe with me."

"I've never understood people drinking coffee in the street," said Blythe. "You don't have an order at a lunch bar?"

"I guess that's where everyone thinks I go," said Con. "But no. Too many people: too close together... Even with the wipe."

"But you walk around outside," said Blythe.

"I wouldn't get through the day if I didn't get a break from Joy."

"Why do you pretend to like her?"

"I don't, not really. I just like company, is all. I like to hear someone talking. I like to sit in a room with people... Not too many, obviously... just someone."

"And that's why you're doing this?"

"It beats walking around the block, and it stretches my brain," said Con. "And you're way better company than a thousand Joys."

Blythe almost spat out her coffee, as she laughed with her mouth full.

"Can you imagine a thousand Joys?" she said.

"I can't imagine a thousand people."

They sat together in silence for a moment.

"You'll check some more of the data tomorrow?" asked Blythe.

"It'd be my pleasure."

They both turned back to their screens, aware that time was well and truly up on their project for the day. Tomorrow couldn't come soon enough. Con wasn't using his private connection, so there were lots of things he couldn't do, including access the internet to check Dharma's data, but he was willing to do this, and he was willing to do it for her. It made Blythe feel good, and it gave her more time to communicate with her newfound relation.

Every day, when she opened her private connection, Blythe found more text from Dharma, more conversation, more details of her life, and of their shared ancestry. Dharma even started to recount some of her grandmother's stories. They were fragmented, incomplete, dragged out of her memory by sheer force of will, but they formed a connection between them, an important connection.

Twelve

When Verity and Sage arrived at the house, all was quiet. There was nobody in the street, although Verity thought she saw some curtain-twitching from the neighbour opposite.

"Hope Savery could never keep her nose out of other people's business," said Verity, gesturing across the street. "She must be going crazy in there, alone with her kids."

Sage looked where Verity was pointing. He smiled, and waved.

"What did you do that for?" asked Verity, smiling.

"Just being neighbourly."

"I bet you've made her day. She'll be on the phone, telling everyone she knows that someone's arrived at the Motts' place... No she won't, she'll be sending out group texts, and posting on the neighbourhood FaceBook page."

"Is that so bad?" asked Sage.

"I suppose it gives her an outlet. You've got to feel sorry for her, really, she's just about the most sociable person I know, by which I mean that she's the nosiest, and the gossipiest."

"Most likely to gossip."

"Nope," said Verity, "I think you'll find gossipiest is a word, and if it wasn't before, it is now. How much do you want to bet me that Pa's phone rings before we're even in the house?"

"I have nothing to wager with," said Sage, turning out his empty trouser pockets to prove it.

"You always have something to wager with," said Verity, looking directly at Sage's crotch.

"We can't!" said Sage. "Not under your dad's roof!"

"Don't sound so shocked, and don't be so damned prim. We're adults. Pa knows the score."

"Well, I'm not sure I'm comfortable with the score," said Sage, as Verity bent over in front of him. "What the hell are you doing, now?"

She stood up, and showed Sage the key she'd got from under the doormat.

"Looking for this," she said.

Verity unlocked and opened the garage door, and, before going in, put the key back under the door mat.

The garage light was already turned on, from inside the house, so Verity pulled the door down until it latched shut. The front part of the garage was separated from the back with a pair of heavy plastic doors. They overlapped where they met and had rubber brushes top and bottom, making seals with the floor and ceiling.

"When did he install this?" asked Sage.

"The doors have been here for years. Pa's a hobbiest, and the front of the garage always used to be full of motorbike parts. The doors were meant to keep solvent smells and spray paints out of the other half, where Mum keeps a spare fridge and washing machine."

"So where's his hobby stuff?" asked Sage.

"It's been less, the past few years, and I haven't been in here for a while. I guess he gave it up. You'd have to ask him." She smiled. "Now, strip off."

"What! Here?"

"Pa's instructions," said Verity.

She laughed at the look on Sage's face.

He jumped as he heard a landline ringing on the other side of the wall.

"I told you Hope would be on the phone before we'd even got in the house. Don't worry. He never picks up the landline."

The phone cut out after four rings, and Sage breathed a sigh.

"Right," said Verity. "Let's get on with it."

The shelves in the front part of the garage were empty, apart from some essential supplies. Verity began to take off her jacket and pull her sweater off over her head, as she picked up a lidded, plastic container. By the time she got back to Sage she was in her bra, undoing the fly of her jeans, balancing the container on her hip with one hand.

"Seriously," she said. "You've got to get naked."

57

She put the box down and took off the lid, pulling out a spray bottle of sanitizer. She squirted some on her hands, spreading it well past her wrists before squirting some on Sage's hands.

Then she pulled out a ziplock bag and some surface wipes.

"For our phones and documents," she said.

"Okay."

A couple of minutes later, everything had been wiped down and was in the ziplock, apart from the paper certificates that they'd been given by the medics. Verity folded these, and put them in another ziplock bag that she slid into the box.

Then she pulled out a thick, yellow, plastic sack, opened it, and started putting her clothes into it. Sage followed suit.

"Good job you put trainers on," said Verity, giving her hands another squirt. When the sack was full of their clothes, Verity tied off the top, and squirted it all over with the sanitiser. She then put their trainers in a second sack and followed the same protocol.

She walked up to the doors, and dropped the sacks on the floor, close to them. Then she put her hand through the water from a hose for a minute or two.

"Clever Pa," she said, and then aimed the hose at Sage, who was holding the ziplock with their phones in it. He hoped it was waterproof.

He put his head down and his arms up, in a defensive posture, until he realised that the water was hot... not just warm, but actually hot.

Verity showered him down carefully, and then handed him the hose so that he could do the same for her. When they were done, they showered down the yellow bags and carried them through the doors. Verity still held the bottle of sanitiser, which she'd also washed down with the hose, and Sage still had the ziplock with the phones and ids in it.

Once they were through the doors, Verity carefully, emptied their clothes into the washing machine, putting the bag in too. She left the bag of shoes on top of the machine.

"I think that worked pretty well," said Sage. "What next?"

Verity doused her hands with sanitiser again, just to be on the safe side, before they dressed in clothes from another plastic box:

joggers and a t-shirt for Verity, and a pair of Pa's pyjamas for Sage. There were also two pairs of slippers, like the ones expensive hotels provided for their guests. There weren't any towels, but Verity and Sage were already virtually dry, apart from their hair. Verity sprayed their feet before they stepped into the slippers. She was convinced that this part of the garage had been thoroughly cleaned and sanitised by her parents, but she didn't want to take any risks. Her parents hadn't, so why would she?

Finally, Verity took the ziplock from Sage, opened it, and took out her phone.

"You can open the door now, Pa," she said, after a moment. She smiled at something he said back to her, and hung up.

Thirteen

Having found her mother's birth certificate, Dharma thought she might have enough information to find her grandmother's. Since her mother had been an only child, and since she didn't trust the male line for genetic matches, Dharma wanted to look for other women in the family, and her grandmother was the next obvious choice. She knew now where she had lived, at least during the Deluge. Perhaps she had been born there, too.

Dharma had pushed her lunch break back, permanently. She enjoyed the longer, uninterrupted mornings, and the short afternoons, after she had done the work that really mattered to her.

Her mother had always acknowledged her own mother's birthday and had always mentioned it to Dharma. She'd even talked about them being born under different astrological signs, even though, their birthdays were less than a fortnight apart. Dharma subtracted the duration of her grandmother's pregnancy from the timeline, and worked out that her grandmother must have been between eighteen and twenty-two if she had been studying for her first degree. She'd begin by breaking it down by year.

"Verity Cornelia Mott," she said. "October fifteenth, 2024, Catford.

+Data not found+

"Correction: October fifteenth 2023."

+Data not found+

She counted down to 2020 with the same negative result each time. Dharma thought that those five years should cover it, but anything could have happened. Her grandmother might already have been pregnant while she was away from home, or she might have begun her degree late. *One more*, she thought.

"Correction: October fifteen 2019."

+Data not found+

If her grandmother had been born in hospital, perhaps it had been in the London Borough of Lewisham, where she lived.

Dharma began again.

"Verity Cornelia Mott, October fifteenth, 2024, Lewisham."

+Data not found+

Undetered, Dharma went through the same years, using Lewisham instead of Catford, until she got to 2019.

The screen blinked, and a birth registration form similar to her mother's came up. She called on the field on the right to view the certificate, and paid the four tix.

Dharma glanced over the document, and then zoomed in for verification. She felt the slightest quaver in her voice as she spoke the command.

The first column was a three digit number, as she'd come to expect. The second column read, 'Fifteenth October 2019', and then, below, 'University Hospital, Lewisham'. Next 'girl', and then her grandmother's name, 'Verity Cornelia Mott'. The next column read, 'Pax Mott', and then came Dharma's great-grandmother's name, 'Faith Melody Mott, formerly Bigelow, of Stannard Court, Culverley Road Catford SE6'.

"Catford, SE6," said Dharma.

+Communication?+

"Negative. Scroll right."

The rest of the certificate showed that Pax Mott had informed the authorities of the birth, and that he had been a pharmacist. He had also informed the authorities, in good time, on the 19th of October, only four days after his daughter had been born.

He had been a pharmacist. *So he was clever*, thought Dharma. She also realised that he would have been well placed to deal with the Deluge. Perhaps some of her grandmother's stories, handed down by her mother, had not been so far-fetched. A pharmacist would know what to do in the event of a pandemic, perhaps not as well as a doctor, but well enough.

Dharma's mind was working fast, and she reacted quickly.

"What was the distance in 2020 between Catford SE6 and Bromley?" Dharma asked. She thought it was a long-shot, but she also knew that old maps were easily available online.

She so badly wanted these people to be her family, but she wanted better assurances. She'd seen a map of the London boroughs but she had no way to judge distances.

A map came on screen, with a red line drawn between Catford and Bromley, both names clearly marked. A box-out read '6.1 miles. 25 minutes', and next to the time was a symbol that resembled some of the cars Dharma had seen in the old movies her mother liked to watch.

Cars moved faster than people could, and Dharma knew that was the point. She also knew that it was perfectly possible to walk six miles. She jogged three miles in a little over half an hour. Dharma's mother and grandmother had been born six miles, or about an hour's jog from the place she had been born and grown up with her mother.

Dharma allowed herself to enjoy a few moments of excitement. She uploaded the certificate to her home screen, and added it as a photo. Then she walked around her cubicle for a few minutes, partly in celebration, and partly to walk off the nervous energy that had welled up inside her.

She stopped suddenly, realising she had been going backwards through the generations. To find a genetic connection who might still be alive, she would have to move sideways and then forwards, looking for relations of the same generation as Verity and their descendants.

Pre-Deluge census records were also in the public domain. Old birth, marriage and death records bore no resemblance to New Wave record keeping, and she wondered whether the same would be true for census records. Her next step should be to find census records for this little family, since she now had names, dates of birth, and even home addresses. She just wasn't sure what the records would tell her.

"Generic census record 2020," she said

+Data not found+

She thought for a moment.

"Generic census record, twentieth century."

A data box appeared on her screen with listings, every decade from 1901 to 1991, always in year one of the decade.

Dharma smiled. "Generic census record 2021," she said.

The first page of a form appeared on the screen.

"Scroll down, continuous."

The screen scrolled for several seconds, at a little faster than reading speed, but Dharma got the gist, and quickly realised that a form like that could give her a lot of very useful data.

It would have to wait until tomorrow, though. Her lunch break was almost over and she didn't want to begin something that she couldn't finish.

Dharma cleared the screen and called up the next page of her latest project. She'd be home in a couple of hours, and could have another look at the certificates she'd uploaded to decide whether she needed more to verify her findings so far. She also wanted to memorise all of the content, so that she wouldn't have to keep referring back to old documents while looking for new ones.

Fourteen

"I wish I'd let you have the extra connection last week," said Con.

"Why?" asked Blythe. "What difference would it have made?"

She was filling out standard invoices on-screen, and the conversation wasn't a distraction.

"All the difference in the World," he said. "If you'd started last week, I could've given you my connection, this week, to keep you in touch with Dharma for longer. We could've learned a lot more with double the time."

"You would've done that for me? What about you?"

"Are you kidding?" asked Con. "This is way more interesting than the stuff I was messing about with. I feel like I wasted that connection. Anyway, I like the data, and I like sorting through it. It beats the day job."

"If you're in the ninetieth percentile, this doesn't have to be your day job."

"No," said Con, "but then I'd be allocated my own cubicle, and I'd go out of my mind if I had to sit in isolation all day and then go home to my flat to be alone some more."

"You really don't like it, do you?"

"I really don't. A few years ago, I had a single cubicle on the second floor for about six months. I had myself demoted to this."

"You couldn't do that job from here?" asked Blythe.

"I was dealing with confidential stuff. I couldn't work in a shared cubicle then, and I can't talk about it now… You wouldn't want to know, anyway."

"And at home?" asked Blythe.

"I don't use my connection at home," said Con. "Mum's dead, and there isn't anyone else."

"But you're so outgoing."

"Not as much as you think. I didn't speak to Joy until she started talking to me. I don't think that woman knows how to stop talking."

"I wouldn't mind so much if everything that came out of her mouth wasn't so negative," said Blythe, "and mostly about me."

"It's been nice, hasn't it, this past week?"

"Yeah. I'm really beginning to think that I might have a relation out there, and even if I don't, Dharma's amazing."

"I meant that it's been nice talking to each other," said Con, "sharing something."

"Oh… Yeah… Sorry. I'm becoming a bit obsessed with all this, aren't I?"

"No, it's Okay. I get it. I'd be excited if it were me."

There was a pause as Blythe got over her embarrassment. "Do you think we'll keep talking to each other after Joy gets back?" she asked.

"She'd hate that. She wouldn't last six months in here if you and I were talking to each other instead of listening to her… Wait… That's starting to sound like a plan."

"You want to force her out?" asked Blythe. "Is that kind?"

"She's had a good run. And I'm not talking about forcing anything. I'm just saying that if you and I were friendly, she might not hang around."

"They'd soon put someone new in with us, and as my mother always says, 'Better the devil you know'."

"But does she ever say, 'A change is as good as a rest'?"

"Actually, no," said Blythe, "but I like that."

"Shall we just decide to keep this going, after Joy comes back?"

"On one condition," said Blythe.

"Anything."

"We don't talk about Dharma in front of her."

"Done," said Con. "We'll just take the same lunch break, and talk about Dharma and her data when Joy's not here."

"There won't be as much to talk about, unless I make a permanent connection to Dharma, and it still feels too soon for that."

"We'd better make the most of today and tomorrow, then."

For the two remaining lunch breaks that week, Blythe and Con got into a routine. He went out for coffee while Blythe uploaded any new data to his screen. Then they sat at their stations, Blythe reading

Dharma's text documents and writing back to her, Con studying the data.

He suggested that Blythe ask Dharma to send across any picture files of the certificates she talked about as text-only files.

"Why should we do that?" Blythe asked.

"It gets me closer to the source material," said Con. "When did you tell her that you have limited capacity?"

"On day one, Monday. She uploaded so much stuff to me that it was clear she has VR, and I wanted to warn her that I was keying in. I didn't want her to think I was being deliberately terse, or that I wasn't interested in her."

"That's why she made data files for you. But she keyed in the files herself, or more likely used her voice recognition, rather than converting the source material to text only files."

"How can you tell?"

"I had a single on the second floor, remember," said Con, over his shoulder. "I might not work for W.W. but I know data, and I know this is copied, not converted from source. It all looks good, but I'd love to compare documents, just to make sure Dharma has accurately transposed the material."

"Okay, I'll ask her."

"If she has capacity, you can tell her to send the new files straight to me if you like."

"But you only have two connections."

"I only use one."

"But that's…" Blythe trailed off.

"I don't have any personal connections," said Con. "I only ever use the service connection."

"So why did you need three connections last week?" asked Blythe, dumb-founded."

"I didn't," said Con. "I'm sorry. I just didn't want you to think I was the loneliest person in SE6d2."

"You don't connect with anyone unless you need some special service, to adjust your tariff, or to fill out your state checks?"

"That's about the size of it."

"That's horrible, but at least I understand now why you're so friendly with Joy."

"She's friendly with me," said Con.

"You were friendly with me," said Blythe.

"And around it goes. This is better, though."

"I should hope so," said Blythe, completing the invoice, and clearing her screen. "It could hardly be worse."

"Just give her my connection details. If she's ninetieth percentile and she's looking for a genetic relationship, I'm guessing that she's got open connections she's not using."

"Okay… I suppose that should be all right."

"Don't worry," said Con. "I might be sociable but Dharma's not looking for me; she's looking for you. I'm not going to muscle in on your relationship."

"I didn't think you would."

"Of course you did. You're just too timid to admit it."

"Or too polite," said Blythe, glancing over her shoulder and smiling. "But you're right, of course I did."

"Another half an hour and we can get onto it," said Con. "Are you on target."

"Right on target. Do you imagine that your chatter slows my work down?"

"Not for a moment."

They finished their morning's work in silence and, when it was time, Con went out for their coffees.

It was Thursday, and they only had two forty minute windows of opportunity to check all the data and read all the material.

After uploading Con's connection details to Dharma, Blythe went back to reading Dharma's stories, and replying with answers to her questions.

"Did you put through my connection details?" Con asked, once he was back at his station.

"No reply yet. It's Friday tomorrow. Time's running out."

"There's nothing left for me to do," said Con.

"I'll upload something to your screen," said Blythe.

A couple of days ago she'd decided not to send any of Dharma's text documents to Con's screen, but things were changing fast. She was beginning to trust Con and would just have to hope that Anley Corp wasn't monitoring the material. Con had an education, and skills that she sorely lacked. Maybe he'd spot something in Dharma's long e-mails that would clarify or verify something in the data. She stopped short for a moment. If it was possible for something in the text to verify the data, then it was equally likely that there'd be something in the text that would contradict the data.

Blythe dreaded the thought.

Then, she sent the first of Dharma's e-mails that Con hadn't already seen to his screen. Either way, it was better to know.

Fifteen

Pax Mott opened the connecting door between the garage and the main house, and stood back.

"Hi, Pa," said Verity, and blew him a kiss.

"Hello, darling. I'm so glad you're home, and I'd kiss you if it wasn't for this damned thing." Pax gestured his gloved hand at his face mask.

"We're clear, Pa, Certified, and everything."

"I know you are, darling, but we aren't. We've been tested but we haven't had the results yet, and the last thing we want to do is infect you. Your mother's with me in our room, and your sister's in the box room, until the results come through."

"That's crazy. You can't live like that. "We're all in this together."

"We'll all be in it together once the results are through," said Pax. "It shouldn't take long. Everything's been sterilised and, until we get the all-clear, I've written up a rota for the kitchen and bathrooms and posted one on each door."

"Why doesn't that surprise me?" asked Verity.

"I'm sorry, son, I should have said hello to you, by now. It's rude of me."

"Not at all, Mr Mott," said Sage, waving.

"Call me Pax. Who knows how long we're going to be housemates for… Too long for all this formality. We're happy to have you here, Sage."

"And I'm happy to be here. Thank you very much for having me."

"You're welcome. And I don't want to hear you thanking me again until all this is over."

"Yes, sir," said Sage.

"Pax."

"Oh leave him alone, Pa," said Verity. "He's nervous enough as it is."

"You two are in the other double," said Pax.

"I bet Charity's thrilled about that," said Verity. "She couldn't wait to take over my room when I left."

"She was a bit resistant, at first," said Pax. "I'm not gonna lie, but, once she realised how serious this whole thing was, she wanted you to come home as much as your mum and I did. She moved into the box room as soon as she knew I'd sent you tickets for the train."

"Well good for her. I thought she might be a brat about it."

"She's seventeen, Verity. She's allowed to be a bit of a brat. I seem to remember you being a colossal pain in the neck at her age... Maybe we won't talk about that in front of Sage, though, eh?"

"By the end of this you'll have shown him every baby picture and told him every sordid story about me," said Verity.

"Can't wait," said Sage, smiling. Verity punched his arm, and Pax's eyes crinkled up as he smiled behind his mask.

"It's bloody good to have you home," he said. "Both of you. You bring some life back into the house. You can help out with Charity's studies, too. Give you all something to do, and maybe your mother can do something about that hair." He gestured again with his gloved hand, but Verity could see that he was still smiling.

"Whatever you say, Pa."

"Well, I'd better get back to your mother," said Pax. "Make yourselves at home, and enjoy the luxury, such as it is. I've put in a form for you two to be included in the food rations, but that won't kick in for a few days. I've stuck rations instructions to the fridge door and the pantry. Once we're all cleared, this is going to be a very busy little house."

Verity blew her father another kiss, and watched him go upstairs. When the bedroom door was opened, she heard her mother's voice.

"Hello, Verity, darling, and Sage. Can't wait to see you."

"Hey, Mum. Love you."

"Hello, Mrs Mott," said Sage.

"It's Faith," said Verity's mum. "Welcome home."

And with that the door closed.

There was a knock on the inside of the box-room door.

"Hey, Chaz," Verity shouted.

"You stole my room," Charity shouted in response.

70

"I'll pay you back."

"You'd better."

They had to shout to be heard through the door, which Charity clearly had no plans to open, but the exchange was light, loving even.

"Seems like my little sister might have turned a corner," said Verity. "She really was a brat when I left home."

"These things change people," said Sage.

"Not us," said Verity. "It'll never change us."

The house was quiet, and Verity and Sage embraced in the hallway.

"What do you want to do first?" asked Verity.

"Sit down," said Sage. "I didn't want to complain, but my feet have been killing me for about the last two miles."

Pax Mott's rotas worked so well that they didn't see any of the family for two days. Everyone ate, and everyone used the bathrooms, and there were latex gloves and packets of surface wipes, which everyone used diligently in the rooms they had to share. Sage and Verity had been assigned the half-bath on the ground floor, which was a tiny wet room; so tiny, in fact, that it was impossible to use the shower and the toilet at the same time, and there was a mixer tap on the wall for hand washing, which had no sink underneath, just a drain in the floor. Sage got used to turning the tap on just enough, and standing at the proper distance, so that he could wash his hands without soaking his clothes or getting his feet wet.

It all worked very well.

On the second day after they'd arrived, Sage was back in his own clothes, and both his and Verity's sneakers were propped against a radiator, drying off from their run in the washing machine.

On the third day, Pa threw open his bedroom door. Faith flew past him, and even Charity managed to make it down the stairs before Pax.

Everyone hugged everyone, including Sage, although he felt a little awkward when Charity put her arms firmly around him.

"So, we're all clear then?" Asked Verity, once they'd all disentangled themselves from each other.

"Well, as it happens, the results are very interesting," said Pax.

"Pa, just enjoy the moment. We're all clear!"

"We're all clear," said Pax. "Like you two, your mother and I have managed to avoid exposure to the pathogen... And this is where it gets really interesting..."

"Don't keep us in suspense," said Verity.

"It was me," said Charity.

"What was her?" Sage asked. "Sorry... What about Charity?"

"At some point, Charity did in fact have the virus, but her antibodies took care of it, and she is now immune. And, before you ask, no, she isn't contagious."

"Wow!" said Verity, raising a hand in a high-five gesture at her sister. "Go you!"

Charity slapped Verity's raised palm.

"You see," said Pax, "there are advantages to having teenage children who want nothing to do with you, who spend every waking hour that they're not at school shut away in their bedrooms doing heaven only knows what."

"Texting, mostly," said Charity.

"You think she got it at school?" Faith asked.

"Probably."

"But the school was closed months ago."

"She must have been in the first wave of those infected," said Pax. "That school trip to London to see that thing... I expect that's when it happened. Some people are a-symptomatic, apparently."

"That's fine," said Charity. "You can all talk about me as if I'm not even here."

"You're the lucky one," said Pax, putting an arm around his younger daughter. "You don't have to worry about any of this any more. You've had it, and you've survived it."

"And you must carry the weight of the entire family into the future when we all die of it," said Verity, dramatically. "You're our genetic link to whatever comes next."

"Thanks for that,"

"She's kidding," said Faith. "No one's going to die."

"Your mother's right," said Pax. "We're all just going to stay home and follow the protocols until the World is done with the Deluge."

"The Deluge?" asked Sage. "That's what they're calling it?"

"Some clever bugger came up with it," said Pax.

"Where have you been all morning?" asked Charity. "It's all over the web."

"We haven't been web-surfing while we refresh our test results page every two minutes," said Verity.

"Fair point."

"TRRNT/41/pan is a bit longwinded," said Pax. "If you stick some vowels in there, you get Torrent. From there, some linguist in the French department at Oxford came up with 'the Deluge'.

"Like he doesn't have something better to do," said Verity.

"School's out," said Sage, "and this sort of thing makes people's names, their careers! Do you think it'll catch on, uh, Pax?"

"It already has," said Pax.

"It's all over the place," said Charity.

"What was his name?" asked Sage.

"Whose name?"

"The guy at Oxford who coined it... What's his name... her name?"

"I haven't a clue," said Pax.

Verity laughed. "Apparently that *isn't* the sort of thing that makes a person famous," she said.

Sixteen

Dharma had decided that her next step would be to check the census for 2021, and use all the criteria she had to hand to fill in the fields.

At two o'clock, she switched to her internet connection and called up the 2021 census form to check the first few fields.

"Census search 2021," she said. "Required fields."

The screen blinked and a form appeared. Dharma filled in what she could.

"Surname: Mott. Address: 131 Engleheart Road, Catford, SE6. Number of residents over sixteen: 2"

The screen quickly changed to another form, a spreadsheet that gave details of household members. Dharma quickly found Mott, and the address was correct. The first name on the form was Pax Mott, and below that, Faith Mott.

Dharma had hoped to be able to read the entire census form for her family, but there was no insert anywhere that would lead her to any kind of certificate she could download. Nevertheless, the form gave her some new details to cross-reference with the birth certificates she had already found.

In 2021, Pax Mott was living at 131 Engleheart Road, he was the head of the household, whatever that meant, he was married, and he was 33, so he must have been born in 1988, or 1987. His occupation was pharmacist, and his place of birth was somewhere called Leeds, that Dharma had never heard of. Everything else added up, so Dharma read the next row of data.

Faith Melody Mott was listed as wife, and the next box had an 'M' in it for married, which seemed redundant. She was 29, so she must have been born in 1991 or 1992. Her occupation was midwife, and her place of birth was Lewisham.

Dharma clapped her hands in delight.

+Communication+

"Negative." Dharma paced the cubicle for a minute or two. She was convinced that this was the right family. She guessed that the couple had met through their professions, and she was excited that at least one of them was from the area where they lived. She hoped that it didn't matter where Pax Mott had come from, and she knew that people had moved around from place to place before the Deluge. It could even be that Leeds was close to Lewisham. If she needed to, she could check that at a later date. More than anything else, she was pleased that Verity's mother would have helped her with the birth of her own mother, Constance. They were clearly a very lucky family… Or perhaps they'd just done everything right during the Deluge; that would tie-in with Pax Mott being a pharmacist.

"Scroll down," said Dharma.

There was another name on the form. It read, 'Verity Cornelia Mott'. Dharma held her breath while she cast her eye across the row of data. She was listed as daughter, unmarried, and aged one.

Dharma needed to know the date of the 2021 census, so that she could verify that this Verity Cornelia had, in fact, been born in October of 2019.

"Scroll up."

Dharma scanned the information at the top of the form, but couldn't find a date. She went back to the facsimile census form for that year, and read the front cover page. It clearly stated that the census form had to be filled in on April 1st. That was almost six months before Verity would have had her second birthday.

Dharma went back to the data and scrolled right. In the final column it said that Verity Cornelia Mott had been born in Lewisham. This tallied neatly with the birth certificate that she had found. No other family members were listed, which was a disappointment. Dharma had hoped that Verity might have had a sibling, a sister; it was her best hope of finding a genetic relation on the female side of her family.

"Pax and Faith were young," she said.

+Communication+

"Negative." She really must stop thinking out loud.

"Census search 2031," she said. "Required fields."

The screen blinked, and a form appeared. Dharma filled in the same data, again.

"Surname: Mott. Address: 131 Engleheart Road, Catford, SE6. Number of residents over sixteen: 2"

She scrolled down the form, and found all the details the same. Verity Cornelia Mott was listed as daughter, unmarried, aged eleven, and this time she had an occupation; she was listed as 'school pupil'.

"Scroll down".

The next row of data came up on the screen.

Dharma read, 'Charity Grace Mott, daughter, unmarried, aged seven, school pupil, born in Lewisham.

"Birth records. Charity Grace Mott, born 2024, Lewisham University hospital."

She hoped the information would be enough.

+Data not found+

"Charity Grace Mott, born 2023, Lewisham University hospital."

The screen showed a new form, similar to the one that Dharma had seen for Verity. The details were correct, so she didn't hesitate to download the original certificate.

"Checkout," she said, and held her id up to make the payment.

She looked at the certificate for long enough to check that it shared the same details as Verity's, before saying, "Upload to home stream. Photo storage."

Dharma had found her first new female relation where she hadn't had to take another step back through the generations. Her mother had never talked about an aunt, but that didn't mean that her grandmother didn't have a sister. The Deluge and the New Wave had split families up. No one lived in groups. All men lived alone, and all childless women lived alone. Dharma wondered what it must have been like for four people to live together, or for men to live with women. It made her feel strange; the way she had felt watching the old movies with her mother. It was a feeling she didn't like.

"Great-Aunt Charity," she said. "Charity Grace Mott... I wonder who you were. I wonder if you ever had a child. I wonder how I'm ever going to find out whether you did."

+Communication+

"Negative."

There were ten minutes before she had to get back to work, and no more research that she could usefully do in the time. Dharma left her cubicle and went out to the coffee machine. She stepped back into the wipe, waited for the ozone smell, and for the interior doors to open, and raised her hand to the concierge, as she always did.

Back in the cubicle, Dharma took a couple of sips of coffee, and logged back on to W.W.'s intranet. She'd be home in less than three hours. She could think about it all, then, and look over the certificates to see what clues she could find to her next step.

Seventeen

The lockdown wasn't so bad. Groceries were delivered to the garage once a fortnight, and there was enough to eat, just. Faith had kept a small vegetable patch and herb garden for years, and there were fruit trees too, so there was always something fresh to eat, alongside the dried goods, tins and cured meats that were staple supplies.

Every six weeks, four swab packs were included with the groceries. Charity didn't need one, since she was immune. The packs were picked up the following day by ambulance, and two days after that the results were posted on the internet. The results were always the same, and they always came as a relief.

It turned out that Charity wasn't a brat at all. She did her share of the chores, almost without complaining, and she spent time in the garden with her mother, who insisted that everyone should get some fresh air. She also spent a lot of time alone in the box room. She always claimed to be doing the schoolwork that was being posted on the internet, and Pax intermittently checked that she was. But she was keeping in touch with her friends, too, via the various forms of social media.

One day she mentioned Able Dole. They'd never been close at school. He was a bit of a geek, and had spent a lot of time watching science fiction movies and playing computer games. It turned out that he was an only child of a single father, and during the lockdown he missed the company of his classmates. His dad was a key worker, so he spent a lot of time shut up at home, alone. He didn't have many friends but Charity had always been gregarious, so, when he joined one of the group chats, she'd started talking to him.

Charity was easily bored by what she called 'girl-talk', and over the past few months, since the lockdown, there had been a lot of that in the group chats. After a while, all the girls could talk about was how little they were eating and how much weight they'd lost.

"Guess how much weight I've lost?" she said to Verity when they were sharing breakfast one morning. Sage was still in bed, and Mum and Pa were in the garage.

"I don't know. Why do you care? And what's with the whiny voice."

"Nothing," said Charity. "It's just they *always* sound so whiny."

"They?" asked Verity.

"I'm bored," said Charity. "All the girls on the group chat can talk about is food, and how thin they're getting."

"Their mums obviously don't garden."

"You were right, though. I don't care what I weigh, and neither should they. It's boring."

"So," said Verity. "You can talk to me."

"Yeah, right, like we're not shut up together all day, every day."

"Okay, but there must be someone else to talk to besides the girls from school."

"Most of the boys have left the group chat... There is this one boy, Able Dole, I've been talking to him a bit. He's a geek, though."

"Yep," said Verity. "And Pa's a geek, and so for that matter is Sage, and you always seem to have stuff to talk about with them."

Charity got up from the kitchen table, taking the bowl of cereal with her.

"Where are you going?" asked Verity.

"To see if Able's in the group chat. I'm bored."

"Good luck with that," said Verity as her sister ran up the stairs and slammed the box room door.

As Verity finished her breakfast she thought about what life had been like when she was seventeen, the ridiculous hierarchy that seemed to exist between the kids in any classroom; she thought about the vain girls, and the bitchy ones, and she thought about the boys. They had seemed alien, but also incredibly attractive... Some of them, at least. Who was dating whom, and who was going to the prom with whom, and who had sex with whom, all seemed terribly important to high school kids. She guessed that some of those things had been important to her, too, at the time.

University was different, more equal. She'd dated quite a lot in her freshman year, and some of the guys had been great, but she hadn't fallen for anyone; at least, she hadn't fallen hard. She'd fallen hard for Sage, and he was the one person she wasn't supposed to fall in love with.

Sage was faculty. He was only just faculty, after completing his PhD in record time, but he'd been a teaching aid to one of her lecturers. She'd only been nineteen, almost twenty, but at twenty-three he wasn't that much older.

They'd talked, and e-mailed, and then they'd dated, but only off-campus. They'd eat, or go to a movie, or sit together in his tiny bedsit, and watch movies. She hadn't talked about him with her friends, and when it came to student housing she opted for the draw rather than nominate preferred room-mates from her friendship group.

They'd been seeing each other for more than a year before anyone found out. There had been rumours. Her friends noticed that she wasn't dating and that she wasn't always available for supper or a drink, or even for late-night cramming sessions.

After their first anniversary, Sage had informed the faculty. They told him that it wasn't their business, unless there was a teacher/student relationship. There wasn't. They'd met when Verity was taking a single-semester option. They had no official connection.

By that time, they were both happy with the way things were, but when her friends asked her questions Verity told them the truth. She'd grown sick of the excuses and the dissembling, and she hated to lie to their faces.

It turned out that no one had known who her lover was but they all suspected she had a secret boyfriend somewhere. Sage was a regular in the faculty, and some of her friends knew him by sight, but they made no judgements... At least, not to her face.

Charity wasn't going to have any of those experiences, and Verity felt sorry for her. It was all rites of passage stuff that everyone should go through. Maybe Charity could find some of that, remotely, through the internet. Social Media was huge, so there were plenty of ways to connect with people, through shared interests or acquaintances, through the online book and movie groups that had quickly sprung up since the schools had been shut down. Verity didn't know what else was out there, but if there were group chats where girls were discussing their diets, then there must be something for everyone.

Verity decided to encourage Charity's connection to Able. It would probably come to nothing, but teenagers needed romance in their lives. They needed to go through crushes and first kisses. They needed to sit up all night and talk nonsense with each other. She'd done it, and now it was Charity's turn.

The next time Verity saw Charity alone was a couple of days later, on the landing outside the bathroom.

"How's it going?" she asked.

"I hope you're not checking in on my education," said Charity. "That's Pa's job."

"Actually, I was checking in on your social life. Did you have that chat with Able?"

"None of your business," said Charity, and flounced into the bathroom, closing the door behind her.

"Hey, I was going in there!" But she didn't care, she'd wait her turn. Verity smiled. Her sister clearly had talked to Able, and she was clearly going to talk to him again. Good for her.

Eighteen

Dharma had a birth certificate for Charity Grace Mott, but she wasn't sure where she could go with it. Perhaps, for now, she'd have to shelve it.

"What about the marriages," she said, back in her office the following day, already signed onto the internet.

+Communication+

"Negative. Facsimile marriage certificates 2000 to 2010."

The screen quickly filled with a certificate from the beginning of the twenty-first century. She didn't know exactly when Pax and Faith Mott had been married, or when her grandparents had been married, but if she had the form of the certificate in front of her, she should be able to upload enough good data, with some good guesses about dates, and possibly come up with something.

Her grandmother had been young when she'd had her mother, and it was during the Deluge, so there was only a small window of time when Verity and Sage might have got married. It was more difficult with Pax and Faith. She assumed that it was probably after they'd finished their professional training, but wasn't sure how long that would have taken. She knew that it had to be before the census that she'd looked at for 2021. She'd work backwards.

"Marriage: Pax Mott, Faith Bigelow, Catford, 2021."

+Data not found+

Dharma repeated the process for 2020. Again, no data was found.

"Stupid!" she said.

+Communication+

"Negative." It crossed her mind that if there was no hospital in Catford there might not be an office where a marriage could be registered.

"Marriage: Pax Mott, Faith Bigelow, Lewisham 2021."

+Data not found+

Dharma decided to give it five years, before trying something else. There was nothing for 2020 or 2019.

"Marriage: Pax Mott, Faith Bigelow, Lewisham 2018," she said.

A form came up on the screen and an insert box on the right. She paid her four tix to see the certificate.

Pax Mott and Faith Bigelow had been married in Lewisham, at the registry office on June 30th 2018, and had both been living at an address in Catford: flat 6, Apex Apartments, Culverly Road, SE6. Their certificate also gave their ages, which tallied with the census forms, and their professions. Pax Mott was listed as a pharmacist and Faith Bigelow as a nurse. It was close enough; perhaps Faith had taken further courses to qualify as a midwife after her nursing training. It seemed plausible.

Perhaps they'd moved before having the girls. If they'd been in a one-bed apartment, they'd need the extra room. She knew that things had been different in the past, that people had moved around before the Deluge. Both the address on the marriage certificate and on the census, three years later, were in Catford. She'd check the distances if she found other anomalies.

What Dharma hadn't expected was that Pax's and Faith's fathers had both been listed on the marriage certificate, along with their professions. Since she was most concerned with the female lines, she looked at Faith's father's name. He was called Ernest Bigelow, and he was a green grocer.

Finding details had become easier, and Dharma wondered whether it might be possible to do more blanket searches. She had worked out that the form of records had probably changed very little during the Deluge, and that the New Wave records were probably only introduced some time later. She decided to try a search for the years between the 2021 census, and her mother's third birthday

"All registrations," she said, "2021 to 2045, containing Pax Mott, pharmacist, Lewisham."

Her screen blinked, and then it blinked again, and again, as the forms piled up. Pax Mott appeared to have records all over the place. Surely they couldn't all be related to *her* Pax Mott.

Dharma sat down, it would take a while to look at each of the certificates in turn. The first forms were for the census, for 2041 and for 2045. There had been a new census relatively soon after the Deluge was over. It made Dharma's flesh crawl when she realised that it was more-or-less intended as a final body count. Both forms had the Mott's address on them, so she paid for them and uploaded them to her photo storage at home. There were a number of professional indexes for Pax's work as a pharmacist, which Dharma glanced at and dismissed, as she did both their birth certificates, which she already had on record.

The last two forms were for marriage certificates which had Pax Mott listed as the father. One was for Sage Tuke and Verity Mott. She paid to look at the certificate, which gave her more information about Sage, and gave the date of their wedding only a couple of months before her mother's birth. Her grandparents were married on June 24th 2042.

Dharma sat back in her chair for a moment, and then looked for more details on the certificate. It shouldn't have been possible for her grandparents to marry during the Deluge. All weddings had supposedly been cancelled after the first few months of the pandemic, once everyone who could be was isolated. Only at the very bottom of the certificate did she find the information she was looking for.

All the participants of the wedding had signed the certificate 'remotely via the internet'.

Dharma was dumbstruck. She wondered why being married was so important to her grandparents. They were together, and they were having a child; marriage seemed redundant.

Her lunch break was over, so she uploaded the certificate to her photo storage at home. She didn't have time to look at the other marriage certificate, but her interest had been piqued by her grandmother's, so she paid and uploaded it, to look at when she got home.

She was answering a lot of questions about her family. She didn't understand all of what she had gathered, but she was piecing together a tree; all she needed to do was fill in more of the branches.

Dharma began to feel as if her search for a genetic relation might actually go somewhere. She really hoped that it would.

Nineteen

+Can we get out of this group chat, and talk on our own+

Charity looked at the message from Able. They'd been talking for a while, but only around other people. They talked books and movies, and school, and they talked about people who weren't in the group chat... Nothing mean, but some of it was funny. Able was funny, and clever, too.

+E-mail me: name, initial, father, year+ She felt sure that Able was clever enough to work out her e-mail address from those clues. He might have to try twice to get the right year, she wasn't sure he knew her birthday.

Her e-mail pinged; he must have got the right year on the first try.

She e-mailed straight back with her phone number, so they could text.

+What's the problem? Pa's a pharmacist, maybe he can help+

+It's the thing... Dad's got it. He got sent straight home from work in a paper suit, mask, gloves, cap... Everything. They incinerated his work clothes, right there+

+You probably don't have it+

+Maybe I don't, but if I'm going to look after Dad, I'll soon get it. Besides... It stands to reason+

+It's all okay... Honestly... I got it at school, in the first wave, and I never even knew there was anything wrong with me+

+It's worse, now. They say it's mutating+

+Stay away from your dad, then, and wait for the next batch of testing+

+No need to wait. Dad had to bring a testing kit home for me. I've already done it. It's being picked up later, and I should know in a couple of days+

+So, stay away from your dad until you know for sure+

+He seems okay, right now... Worried, but okay. I don't have to stay away from him, because he's staying away from me+

+Good. That's what he's supposed to do+

+I know it sounds stupid, but I'm scared+

+It's not stupid… It'd be stupid if you weren't scared+

+They left boxes of gloves, masks, and about a gallon of sanitizer. I've done the whole house+

+Even less likely you'll get it then. You're gonna be fine+

+You make me feel better+

+It'll be okay. You're young and fit, and you've been isolated for a while+

+I'm more worried about Dad. He's been working a lot of shifts. He's tired, and run down. He's lost weight, too+

+Everyone's lost weight… You've been in the group chat… All those stupid girls talking about their gorgeous bodies+

+You're gorgeous+

+I haven't lost any weight. My mum grows food+

+I don't care what size you are… I'm… Can I say that I'm crazy about you, or is that too corny+

+It's too corny… I like it though+

+Gotta go check on Dad, if he'll let me+

+Keep your distance from him, and use the protocols. Stay in touch. Text me any time… all the time+

+Promise+

+Quite like you, too X+

Twenty

"It's Friday," said Con, as he walked back into the cubicle with two cups of coffee. He put one down on Blythe's workstation.

"Yeah," said Blythe.

"The last day before Joy comes back and we lose that extra connection."

"I know," said Blythe.

"Is something the matter?"

"I just want to do as much as I can for the next forty minutes. I can't seem to be able to read or write fast enough."

Con sat at his station and checked his connection. He whooped and threw his arms in the air, making Blythe jump. She turned her chair to face him.

"What?" She asked.

"She's only gone and done it. Dharma's acknowledged my connection request and sent me text files from source!"

"That's…"

"That's brilliant!" said Con. "I can cross reference all the data, and we can be sure… At least as sure as we could ever be."

"That *is* brilliant," said Blythe. "But what if you find an anomaly?"

"Then, we'll have to satisfy ourselves that at least you and I have formed a friendship over the past week."

Blythe turned her chair back to her station.

"Yeah," she said.

"You're disappointed," he said. "It's okay, I'm used to being a disappointment.

"I know you want this connection," he continued. "I know you want her to be your… what? Some sort of cousin, I suppose, but you can't make it your whole life."

"Why not?" said Blythe, still keying in as she spoke to him. "She's made it her whole life, probably for weeks and weeks. She's done all the work. Maybe she needs this even more than I do. I don't want either of us to be disappointed."

"You won't be. You've made a connection with her, neither of you is going to give that up, even if it turns out that you don't have a genetic relationship."

"It would be amazing, though."

"It would, and I'm going to spend some time trying to verify that for you, right now."

"Thanks," said Blythe, breaking off for a moment to smile at him.

"You do have a lovely smile," he said

The smile turned to a scowl.

"Just saying."

While he was working, Con took screen shots of the data, and uploaded them to his photo storage at home. It would give him something to do over the weekend, and, maybe, on Monday, he'd have some concrete news for Blythe, one way or the other.

Since their conversation the day before, Con had been thinking a lot about the value of connections. He didn't value them at all. He had a connection that was permanently free, and he never used it, and had never assigned it. Most people who had mothers used their primary connections to keep in contact with them, often on a daily basis. He was fully aware of Joy's connection to her mother, since the relationship was one of Joy's favourite topics of conversation, and often wondered why she kept the connection going, since she never did anything but complain about it. But, that was Joy.

Con had used his primary connection to request a connection with Dharma, who clearly had a lot of capacity. She must work alone, and she must live alone, and she obviously wasn't in contact with her mother. It stood to reason. Dharma obviously had an open internet connection, and she'd been using a connection exclusively for Blythe for the past week. Now she'd opened one up to Con that clearly didn't reduce her capacity.

If that was the case, and he was almost sure it was, he'd leave the connection to Dharma open and see if she chose to close it. If the connection was still open when he got back to work on Monday morning, he could do even more for Blythe.

He liked her. He admitted it. He admitted it to himself, and he'd paid Blythe enough compliments for her to know that he liked her. She might become his first genuine friend. They could share jokes and stories, and just talk to each other about stuff, at least during office hours. He didn't want to give that up, and he hoped that Joy wouldn't get in the way of it. No, whatever happened he wouldn't allow Joy to get in the way of his friendship with Blythe.

"What happens on Monday?" Con asked, as they both switched their screens back to Anley Corp data.

"I don't know," said Blythe. "How far did you get, checking the documents?"

"There are a lot to check. It's going to take me a while."

He saw how crestfallen she was.

"Sorry," he said. "At least all the data's downloaded, so we can take a look at it together, next week."

"I just won't be able to send and receive e-mails directly with Dharma," said Blythe

"Unless you give her one of your connections."

"I would, but there's a thing."

"What kind of a thing?" Asked Con.

Blythe hesitated.

"You don't have to tell me," he said. "You use that connection two weeks out of three to talk to someone."

"Not really," said Blythe. "It's just someone I used to work with. He was kind to me, and, after he retired, he was moved to a senior's place. He's lonely, is all."

"Funny, a nice smile, and kind," said Con, "although you'd never know it by the way you treat me."

Blythe batted at him with her hands, but didn't touch him.

"I treat you the way you deserve."

"So, we're not friends, yet, then?"

"Of course we're friends. Do you think I'd trust you with all this stuff if we weren't friends?"

"Yes, I think you would," said Con, "because you're desperate, and you need me."

"Fair point," said Blythe, and they smiled at each other.

They went back to work for the rest of the day, but all the time, Con was hoping that Dharma really didn't have anyone, and that she'd keep the connection open between them.

If Blythe couldn't talk to her, Con certainly could.

Twenty-one

Verity hit the refresh button on her latest test results. They were delivered, alphabetically, by household, and she knew that her parents had already had theirs. They were clear. Charity no longer needed to be tested, because she'd survived the Deluge.

She waited a moment and then hit the refresh button again. The results came up, but she was distracted by a large red box-out, halfway down the screen, so she didn't see whether she had tested positive for the pathogen.

She turned pale, and could feel sweat beads forming under her arms.

"Sage," she called. "Sage!"

Pax heard the cry, and then heard Sage thundering up the stairs. Then Faith and Charity both appeared.

"What's going on, Mum?" Charity called down the stairs.

"No idea," said her mother, as she went up, with Pax following her.

"Are you okay, darling?" Pax asked through the bedroom door, which Sage had closed behind him.

"It's fine," Sage told Verity. "The important thing is that you're healthy. You haven't been exposed to the pathogen."

"Yeah, that's good," said Verity.

"I shouldn't really be in here until I get my results," said Sage.

"I need you," said Verity.

"It's just a formality, anyway. We all live pretty close together, so, if everyone else is clear there's no chance I've got it."

"No. But what about this?" she asked, pointing at the box-out. "This can't be true."

Charity put her ear against the door, trying to hear what was going on inside.

"Charity!" said her father, and the teenager backed away.

"Well, something's going on, Pa, and if it affects us, we ought to know about it."

"Give them a minute," said Pa. "They're allowed some privacy."

Two or three minutes later, Pa knocked on the bedroom door.

"If you two are okay, I'm going to go and put the kettle on. Come down when you're ready."

"Thanks, Pax," said Sage, loudly enough to be heard by the little gathering on the landing.

"Come on, you two," said Pax, ushering his wife and daughter down the stairs. "Whatever it is, we'll all feel better for a nice cup of tea."

"I can't believe you've been a pharmacist for decades and you still believe in the restorative properties of tea," said Faith.

"Tell me I'm wrong," said Pax, walking into the kitchen, and filling the kettle.

"You're not wrong," said Faith. "Stop twitching, Charity; if there's something going on we'll all know about it soon enough."

"I'll make a pot," said Pax.

"Clearly, the government is testing for more than just the pathogen," said Sage.

"But what if it's true?" asked Verity.

"Could it be true?" asked Sage, smiling at Verity, and putting his arms around her.

"Check your status first, while I try to work it out."

Sage reached across Verity, and called up his own medical forms. He refreshed the page twice, and his new results showed up on the second click.

"All clear," he said.

Verity threw her arms around his neck.

"We knew I would be," said Sage. "It's hardly a surprise."

"I'm happy, though. I won't have to go through this without you. You have to stay healthy! You have to promise me."

"I'll do my best," said Sage.

"Swear!" said Verity.

"Okay, I swear... You think it's true?"

"Things have been really complicated," said Verity. "The isolation on campus, then coming back here... I've just realised how much time has passed."

"Tell me about it. It's almost April already. I promised I'd help Faith with all the spring planting, and weeding. We're doing a lot more, this year."

"I didn't mean it like that," said Verity. "I meant, I didn't realise I was past my renewal date."

"Your renewal date? For your contraceptive implant?"

"I should have had it at least six weeks ago, maybe longer. I'm so sorry, Sage. I should never have let this happen."

Sage scooped her up in his arms again, and kissed her.

"You know what that means?" he said.

"That I'm pregnant?" Verity asked.

"No... Well, yes. But it also means we'll have to get married."

"You're excited?"

"We should both be excited. We're going to have a Deluge baby. What could be more perfect than that? What could be more perfect than repopulating the Earth with gorgeous babies... *our* gorgeous babies?"

"Oh God!"

"What?" said Sage, suddenly concerned, cupping Verity's face in his hands. "What, V?"

"Babies," said Verity. "I really hope it's only *one* baby."

Pax, Faith and Charity, had drunk their tea, and Pax had topped up the pot. Two empty mugs sat on the table, while they waited for Sage and Verity to come down the stairs.

"Do you think one of them's sick?" asked Charity.

"No," said Pax. "Not possible."

"Do you think they're splitting up?" asked Charity. "Do you think one of them's cheating?"

"Don't be silly," said Faith. "How could they possibly cheat when we're all in isolation together?"

"The internet," said Charity. "People talk on the internet, they make friends, one thing leads to another, and before you know it, they're having remote sex."

"Charity!" said Pax.

"The Deluge has made stuff real, Pa, you'd better get used to it."

"I'm sure no such thing has happened," said Pa. "You've seen them together. They're happy and playful, and they don't fall out very often. They're cooped up here with the three of us, and limited privacy, and they still seem happy to me."

"You like to see the best of everything, Pa."

"While preparing for the worst," said Faith.

"You see. Mum agrees with me."

Pax started to pour more tea into Faith's mug.

"That's it," said Charity, "I'm going up there before you drown me in tea."

She ran up the stairs, before either of her parents could talk her out of it. They were both anxious to know what was happening, and Pa was already dreaming up contingency plans, in case something was going wrong with his lockdown.

Charity knocked on the door.

"Hey, V, what's going on? You need to come down, Pa's drowning us in tea, and I can't stand it… And I've got to pee!"

"Go pee, then," said Sage. "We'll be down in a minute."

"Promise?" asked Charity.

"Promise," said Sage.

Verity wiped her eyes, and ran her fingers through her hair, which had grown out curlier since her mother had cut it for her.

"Do I look okay?" she asked.

"Beautiful as ever," said Sage. "Now let's get downstairs, you know how Charity is about promises."

"Okay." She took a deep breath and let it out. "Okay."

Charity was walking back into the kitchen as they came down the stairs.

"What's the matter?" she asked. "Why have you been crying?"

"Sit down, Charity," said Pa, pouring tea for Verity and Sage. "I'm sure they'll tell us all about it."

Once the five of them were sitting around the table, Verity squeezing Sage's hand under it, Sage began.

"First of all," he said. "You should know that we're all still healthy. We both tested clear.

"The bad news's coming," said Charity, putting both elbows on the table, and cradling her face.

"Actually," said Sage. "It's good news... We're engaged, we've decided to get married."

Faith stood, and reached across the table to hug Verity.

"Congratulations," she said. "That's lovely."

"It is lovely," said Pa. "Of course it is, but are you planning a long engagement, or should we be looking at the logistics of a Deluge wedding?"

"We'll be having a short engagement," said Verity. "We're getting married because I'm pregnant, and apparently Sage is more old-fashioned than I thought."

Everyone stood, and everyone made a lot of noise, all of a sudden.

"Hold it!" yelled Sage, waving his arms at right angles to his body to signal that people should be quiet.

"We're not getting married because Verity's pregnant," he said, as everyone quietened down. "We're getting married, because we love each other. I just want to make that clear... Now you can make some noise."

Twenty-two

Dharma checked Sage and Verity's marriage certificate when she got home. She found it hard to believe that they'd managed to have any kind of wedding during the Deluge, but clearly they had. There was the certificate to prove it. She could hardly be more sure that these really were her grandparents, and that her grandmother's tall stories had proven to be true.

Not for the first time, Verity wished that she could remember more of the stories, more of the details that would fill the gaps. She wished she'd listened more to her mother, but from a kid's perspective her mother had lived too much in the past, in things that Dharma didn't know about or understand or have any interest in.

She understood her mother much better now than she ever had. She wished she could tell her that. It didn't matter; they'd had a good relationship. They'd loved each other.

Dharma turned to the second marriage certificate. It was for Charity Grace Mott and a man called Able Dole. The address wasn't Engleheart Road, but it was Catford SE6. They had been married on the 10th of March 2043.

Surely that couldn't be right.

Dharma looked again at Charity's birth certificate. She was born in September 2023. She couldn't possibly have got married at the age of nineteen. It seemed crazy. This couldn't be the right girl. Dharma had to have made a mistake somewhere along the line.

She checked the details on the marriage certificate, and Pax Mott was listed as Charity's father, and he was listed as a pharmacist. Surely, there couldn't be two pharmacists called Pax Mott in Catford in 2043. Charity's name was also there, in full, on the certificate, and her age was given as nineteen. The boy, Able Valor Dole, was also only nineteen years old.

Dharma had no idea about marriage, but she was shocked that children who should still be downloading school could be married.

She closed the screen. This would take some thinking about.

To apply for parenthood in the New Wave, women had to be thirty years old, and had to have completed at least ten years in the workforce. Most women didn't finish their educations until they were at least twenty; generally twenty-one-or-two was the minimum for a full education up to a first degree. Some women opted to take higher qualifications, as Dharma had. She'd been twenty-five before she'd gone to work, and at thirty-five she only just qualified to have a child. She had no intentions of doing so yet. She still felt young to be a mother. Her own mother hadn't had Dharma until she was forty-two, and that wasn't considered too old. Most women had only one child, but, depending on the birthrate and the balance of the population in the gender-split, some had a second. After the age of forty-five, women had to undergo rigorous health checks, so the window of opportunity was limited.

Her grandmother, Verity Tuke, gave birth while she was still in her twenties. That could never happen now. She'd been married at twenty-two and Constance had been born within a fortnight of Verity's twenty-third birthday.

It took a lot for Dharma to wrap her mind around all of that. The Deluge had happened years ago. Generations had been born since, who had no connection with the event that had changed the World.

They thought nothing of it. They lived their lives according to the New Wave laws and way of life. It was second nature.

Dharma knew, everyone knew, that things had changed. The Deluge was part of the compulsory history program, but knowing that something had happened and understanding it were two very different things. Besides, the World had been described as a terrible, corrupt, rotting place before the Deluge. The Pandemic had killed a lot of people, but Dharma had learned that it had saved a lot of souls, including her own.

A hundred years before the Deluge there had been a World War. Dharma had taken an optional school download about that, too, but it felt like a story to her. Surely all those terrible things, the war and the holocaust, couldn't possibly have happened the way the school download had described. The people who had been part of it seemed alien beings to Dharma. People could never do such terrible things now, surely. People would never be allowed to commit such atrocities. It couldn't happen under the New Wave regime.

Time and distance had felt like small, finite things to Dharma, until she began her search for a relation. Time was a day in the cubicle or, at most, the duration of a work project. Distance was the short walk to work or, at most, the three mile jogs she took at the weekend.

Time was the duration of her own life, and the duration of her mother's life, but even Constance hadn't been able to tell Dharma much about what the Deluge had really been like, how people's lives had really changed. She'd been born at the end of it, and, by the time she could walk and talk the New Wave had begun. She didn't even remember the changes in her own young life. All she had were her grandmother's stories, and, by the time her mother was telling them to Dharma they were already half a century old.

Dharma's analytical mind told her that unrecorded data like stories, told and retold, must change with time. Elements of the story must be forgotten or exaggerated. No domestic records were in the public domain. There were no diaries or letters. There was only what had been passed verbally from Verity to Constance and then on to Dharma.

The Deluge was open for academic study, mostly of a scientific nature. Personal records of the survivors were not in the public domain, and would not be until a century after the event. Dharma could not wait another twenty-plus years to delve into the domestic lives of people who were long-dead.

Dharma wanted to make a connection, now. More than that, she wanted to make a connection in the present. The past was a strange and dangerous place. All that mattered was today, and tomorrow, and next month. All that mattered was the time that it would take for Dharma to complete her project and find a genetic connection to a living woman.

Dharma walked through the wipe and into the bathroom to wash and change for her jog. Perhaps it would settle her mind, but she decided to take a familiar route rather than see new places or new people. Perhaps today would be the day that she ran to her mother's last home. She didn't know what she'd do when she got there, and she knew that it would actually be a six mile jog, because she'd have to turn around and come home again.

She thought about those six miles between Catford and Bromley on the old map that she'd looked at, and decided that it really wasn't very far. If she needed to walk the three miles home, she could manage it without any problems.

Twenty-three

+Let me know how you are... I'm worried about you+

+I'm fine, honestly, Charity... I've got the rash, but only a little, on my legs. Dad's covered in it, and he won't eat+

+Are you staying away from him, or is it too late for that?+

+It's too late. I've got symptoms. I think he likes having me close to him, but I know he feels guilty that he's given me this horrible thing. The past month has been hard on both of us, trying to isolate from each other+

+I know, Abe. At least, now you can be together more+

+Dad's medication might have slowed down the virus, but I don't think he's going to get through it+

+They're coming up with new drugs all the time+

+What if I have to be medicated?+

+You'll get through it, Abe. You're young, and you're strong... I got over it without even knowing that I had it. I know you'll get better!+

+That's the plan. I'm more worried about Dad than me. He was a key worker, and it doesn't matter what precautions they take, they're in danger all the time from this thing+

+I bet your dad's more worried about you than he is about himself, Able+

+He is. He keeps making me show him my rash, to make sure it isn't getting any worse+

+Is it getting worse? I'm really worried+

+Don't worry, Charity, it's been the same for a couple of days... maybe even less bad... It's nothing+

+I didn't know you'd had it a couple of days... Why didn't you tell me?+

+I didn't want to worry you+

+Is that why you didn't text me at the usual time today? Is that why I had to text you?+

+I was trying to give Dad something to eat, but all he seems to manage is some weak black tea+

+Please look after yourself. I don't know how I'd cope without you. And if he doesn't want them, eat your dad's rations, you'll need to keep your strength up!+

+Anything you say, Charity. I like that you're worried, but I'm fine... You've got your whole family around you, so you'll be fine, too, whatever happens... Now, let's talk about something else... Something a bit more cheerful+

+It's crazy, here... I wasn't supposed to tell you, but things are moving along, so I think it's safe to talk about it now... Besides, you were talking about how I've got my whole family around me+

+Safe to talk about what? Now you've got me worried+

+It's fine, exciting even. Verity's going to have a baby, and she's going to marry Sage+

+You're right, that is crazy! Tell her congratulations from me!+

+I will. Verity's being a bit sarcastic, but Mum says that's just the hormones talking. Her and Sage are very loved-up, it's almost unbearable to watch+

+You've got me... Maybe that'll be us one of these days... You never know+

+What are you saying, Able?+

+The same thing I'm always trying to say to you... I've said I'm crazy about you a million times+

+Maybe not a million... and I quite like you, too+

+That's what we always say to each other, though, isn't it? It might just be because I've got this thing, and because Dad's sick, but I really want you to know that I love you+

Able's screen stalled for several seconds.

+I love you too... I just worry that we're young, and we can't see each other+

+We talk to each other for hours every day... We could hardly be closer+

+What if you don't like me in person?+

+You looked all right to me when we were in school together+

+I didn't know you noticed+

+You're the sort of girl everyone notices, Charity+

+I'll take that as a compliment... But you don't know that I still look the same way I did then. This thing changes people+

+The physical is just the physical. I know you better than I know anyone+

+Even your dad?+

+I love my dad, but it's different with parents... They have their own stuff going on... Don't you feel as if you know me better than anyone?+

+Yeah, I suppose I do. I know you better than I know my best friend, who isn't really my best friend any more, because you are... I know you better than Verity, or Mum or Pa. Sage is nice, and he's almost like a brother, now, but he's got Verity+

+The physical thing doesn't matter then... If we have it one day, that'd be great, but I feel like you're everything I need+

+Well remember that, so that you can get well... You have to get well! That way, we can both be immune, and then... Who knows what might happen+

+I'll get working on that+

Able's screen stalled for a couple of seconds. Then Charity texted again.

+As far as the physical thing... There is stuff we could do+

Charity's screen stalled for a few seconds, and her face began to flush. She couldn't wait any longer for a text, but she didn't know what to say.

+???+

+Sorry, Charity, I'm here... I just...+

+Just what?+

+That would be exciting... wouldn't it?+

+I just thought we could maybe talk about what we'd like to do together... you know+

+Would you do that, Chaz?+

+I'd like to try, but maybe it's weird+

+I don't think it's weird at all...+

+Later, then... Maybe when your dad's gone to bed+

+He's in bed all the time+

+You know what I mean... Later+

+Maybe when your dad's gone to bed... LOL+

+Yeah… LOL+
+I love you Charity+
+You already said that+
+Well, I'm saying it again+
+Bye Able… Love you+
+Bye Charity… Later!+

Twenty-four

"Are you taking the supplements we ordered, Verity?"

"Are you my midwife, Mum?" Verity asked.

"Looks like it," said Faith.

"It does, doesn't it? I hope that doesn't mean you're going to do a lot of poking about and stuff... Bit embarrassing for both of us."

"You haven't got anything I haven't seen before, hundreds of times."

"But this time it's me."

"Then I guess we'd both better get used to it," said Faith. "But the answer to your question is that, no, I won't be doing a lot of poking about. I'll check your pee and take your blood pressure, maybe keep an eye on your weight."

"Sounds easy enough," said Verity, relieved.

"I'm just happy I've got my own kit: blood pressure cuff, urine testing strips... you know?"

"No, Mum, I don't really know, but if you've got it sorted I'll leave the worrying to you."

"You should tell me if you have any symptoms or sensations you haven't had before. And I've got an old scope somewhere that I can sterilise, so that I can check the baby's heart-rate, and a tape measure to make sure he's growing."

"How on Earth are you going to measure a baby that's inside me?"

"By running a tape from the top of the bump to your pubis."

"Okay, that's too much information. And how can you magically tell that it's a 'he'?"

"There's no magic in childbirth, and I don't have an ultrasound kit... Maybe I could get one."

"Did mothers and babies survive in a time before ultrasound was invented?" asked Verity. She had a bent for the sarcastic during the first phase of her pregnancy, when she felt unsure about a lot of things and felt nauseous for at least half of her waking hours.

"I don't think we need to worry about an ultrasound machine, Mum. Unless you think that things aren't going well."

"So far, so good," said Faith.

"Good."

"If we're still in lockdown when it's time for the birth, how much do you know about all of that?"

"I'm guessing you know enough for both of us, Mum, but I'm determined to have this baby in a nice, clean hospital, so the Deluge had better be over by then. It should be at least another five months, maybe even six, before the baby comes."

"It's a shame we don't have more accurate dates," said Faith, "but it'll come when it's ready."

"Now my baby's an 'it'?"

"If we got an ultrasound kit, I could tell if it's a boy or a girl,"

"No ultrasound kit, Mum. Besides, it could be born one gender and grow into an entirely different gender. The World isn't binary, you know."

"That's very true. We all get what we're given. Whoever they turn out to be, I'm sure they'll be wonderful."

"Thanks, Mum," said Verity, putting her hand on her belly even though there wasn't really a bump yet, just a thickening of her waist. "We should talk about the wedding. Do you know if Pa's found anything out?"

With that, her father walked into the room.

"Did I hear my name spoken in vain?" he asked, smiling.

"I was just wondering whether you'd found out anything about the wedding?" said Verity.

"As a matter of fact I've just called Sage in from the garden… I'm sure he'll finish up afterwards, Faith… I just thought you should hear this together."

"So either it's good news, and you can enjoy it together or it's bad news and you can console each other," said Faith.

"No need to explain," said Verity. "We all know how Pa's mind works."

"You couldn't be a little less sarcastic, I suppose?" asked Pa.

"It's a phase," said Faith. "The first trimester… all those hormones whizzing around, and the nausea… Leave her alone."

"She could at least try," said Pa.

"She's doing her best," said Faith.

"I am, Pa," said Verity. "Love you."

Sage wandered into the living room in his stockinged feet. He'd left Pa's wellies outside the back door. They were a size too big for him, so he was wearing two pairs of socks, and his jeans were tucked into the top pair.

"I see why I love you so much," said Verity. "You're SO attractive."

"It's just the sarcasm," said Sage. "She's not actually having a go at me... This is just her thing right now." He smiled at Faith and Pa.

"It seems so," said Pa.

"What can I do for you, Pax?"

"You can sit down, and I'll tell you what I've found out about this wedding."

Sage sat, his expression more serious. He seemed braced for disappointment.

"It turns out that you can get married," said Pa.

Sage beamed.

"You can dress up, and have a wedding breakfast and everything... A proper celebration!"

"That's great, Pa, but what's the downside?" asked Faith.

"No downside. It'll just have to be a small wedding."

"How small?" asked Faith.

"Well, when you think about it," said Pa, "the only people that really matter are you and Sage."

"I'm not getting married without my family," said Verity. "It's bad enough that Sage's parents can't be here."

"They're fine with it. They're just excited to be grandparents."

"Great," said Pa. "Then you'll be delighted with the current arrangements for Deluge weddings."

"Just tell them," said Faith.

"You mean, tell you," said Pa, smiling.

"My daughter's getting married, so yes, I'd quite like to know something about the arrangements."

"The Registrar's office in Lewisham is performing remote weddings," said Pa.

"What does that mean?" asked Faith.

"It means marriage by e-mail," said Verity, still sarcastic.

"Actually, we set a date," said Pa, "and we do the wedding live by Zoom, so that we can see the registrar, and she can see us. We've already been assigned someone… I took the liberty, because there's a waiting list of about six weeks… She's called Harmony Kimmel… Great name for a registrar."

"Well, that's something, at least," said Faith.

"We can do it here… Set up in the living room, get dressed up," said Pa, excited. "We can even have your parents hooked up via Zoom, Sage, so they can see what's going on."

"We'd better make it soon," said Faith.

"The baby isn't due for a while. There's plenty of time," said Sage.

"You're not crapping out on me, are you?"

"Of course not, V. I'd marry you tomorrow."

"That might be a bit soon for the registrar," said Pax. "Like I said, we're looking at closer to six weeks."

"Verity," said her mother. "I just thought you might like to wear my wedding dress. I could make some alterations to it, if it's not to your taste, but it's still packed up in the back of the wardrobe. It might be nice for it to see the light of day, one last time."

"Do you think it'd fit?" asked Verity.

"I think so, if we don't put off the wedding for too long. We could go and try it on if you like, and make the alterations nearer the time."

Verity got up from the sofa for the first time that day, and she and her mother were soon upstairs, unwrapping the old wedding dress and taking stock.

"So," said Pax, "do you have a preferred date, Sage?"

"Whenever suits you."

"Talking of suits, you could wear one of mine. You'll have to have a chat with Faith about alterations, but I'm sure we can sort you out."

"Thank you. If Verity's in a dress, it'd be nice to look a bit smart."

"We'll all dress up," said Pax. "But, about that date?"

"The sooner the better," said Sage.

"I'll get right on it, then."

"I'll finish that bit of gardening."

"Good lad." Pax, rested his hand on Sage's shoulder. "Good lad."

They both knew that Pax wasn't talking about the gardening.

Twenty-five

+That was…+

+I know… I don't know what I expected, but we should definitely do that again+

+I love you, Charity, and we can do that any time you want+

There was a short pause.

+Are you okay, Abe?+

+I'm better than okay. I'm happy, and tired+

+Why are you tired?+

+You take a lot out of a man+

+So… You're a man now, are you?+

+I'm pretty sure you just made a man out of me, Chaz+

+Seriously, though, are you okay? I'm still worried about you+

+I'm fine. The rash is the same. I haven't got any other symptoms. My appetite's fine… In fact, I could eat, right now+

+Good. Go eat something when we've finished talking+

+Yeah+

There was another short pause.

+What is it, Abe?+

+I'm really worried about Dad… He's not getting any better, and he still won't eat. I keep trying to feed him something, but he just doesn't want it. I'm afraid if he doesn't eat he'll only get worse. The medication doesn't seem to be working at all any more+

+When do you get the next test?+

+Every forty-eight hours now… Both of us+

+Okay… And you're doing everything you're supposed to?+

+When the last test came back there was a note on it about an anti-viral drug that they're testing on some patients. They might give it to Dad+

+Well, that's good, isn't it?+

+It's a test drug. They don't know if it works, and I'm worried about Dad being a guinea pig… What if it makes him worse?+

+It's got to be better than the stuff he's taking now... Who knows? It could be the miracle drug they're looking for+

+They're testing Dad's viral load to see if he qualifies+

+I'll be keeping my fingers crossed. Honestly, Abe, it's got to be better than doing nothing+

+I hope so+

+I promise I'm here, whatever happens. Love you, Abe+

+I love you too+

+Go and eat something, and text me in the morning+

+Normal time?+

+Any time. Look after your dad first. I'll be here+

+Thanks, Charity. Love you. Sleep tight+

+Don't let the bed bugs bite+

Twenty-six

Dharma jogged to her mother's old address. An apartment complex, low and sprawling over two floors, it was a lovely place, set in a large garden with lots of companion planting: flowers, vegetables, fruit trees. It looked glorious.

Dharma held her id card up to the scanner at the gate. She wasn't sure it was still valid, but the gate opened and she walked through. If she could get around the side of the building she'd be able to look up at her mother's apartment.

The air was full of the scent of growing things, green and sappy, but also sweet from the abundance of spring flowers and fragrant with the smell of herbs.

Dharma walked through the grass, never mown shorter than ten cm, and around to the rear of the building. Someone, ten or twelve metres away, covered from head to foot in protective clothing, was tending to a beehive. No one was at any risk.

Dharma sat in the grass and looked up. Her mother's apartment had been third from the left on the upper floor. The window box was still there, and somebody was obviously tending to it. The curtains were new. The two neat rooms and the little wet room that her mother had occupied were being lived in by someone else.

It was inevitable; time had passed. It would soon be two years since Dharma had last seen her mother. She was happy, though. The place looked good. Someone new was looking after it, and enjoying it. Everything was okay.

Dharma walked a little further around the building, stepping away so that she could see it as a whole. She brushed against something growing close-by, and was suddenly back at her own flat. What was that smell?

Dharma bent down, and brushed her hands through a patch of purple-blue flowers, they were simple blooms; each had five petals with veins a deeper shade of purple-blue, and pale centres. The leaves were fragile, frilly things. The smell, though… The smell was like the smell of the wipe in her apartment building.

Dharma picked a few of the flowers, plucking them off with long stems, so that she had some of the leaves, too. She walked back to where the beekeeper was finishing up her work for the day, her headgear under her arm. She was a young woman, with warm brown skin, and dark brown eyes.

"Excuse me," said Dharma, keeping a few metres distance from the stranger. "Do you know what these flowers are called?"

"They're geraniums," said the woman. "I'm sorry, do I know you?"

"No. I'm Dharma Tuke. My mother, Constance, used to live here."

"Up there," pointed the woman, "at the back. She had one of the prettiest window boxes."

"That's right," said Dharma.

"I'm Patience Opie," said the woman. "I'm the gardener, here. I knew your mother quite well. She liked it out here."

"I didn't know," said Dharma. "She didn't say."

"She talked about you. How clever you were, how solitary… She worried about you, I think."

Dharma smiled.

"Yes," she said. "She told me how much she worried about me."

"Are you okay?"

"I'm very okay. I just wanted to look at the place, one last time. I wonder why she didn't talk about the garden."

"Aren't you the indoors type?" asked Patience, smiling.

"I suppose I am. These… I like these," she said, holding out the geraniums again.

"Take them, and come back any time. It's good to be outside."

"Thank you, I will… You called them Geraniums?"

"That's right. Do you have space for a window box?"

"I suppose so," said Dharma.

"If you want to get one set up, I'll give you some seeds, and you can grow some… Other things, too, if you like."

"Thank you, Patience," said Dharma. "I might just do that."

Then she waved, and walked back to the gate for her jog home, still holding the flowers. She smelt them again. It was a safe smell, the smell of home. Maybe she would install a window box. She didn't want to live in the past, but if her mother had liked plants perhaps she'd do it for her.

She thought about it as she jogged home. She hadn't ever opened her windows, and she didn't know whether she could, or should. Every building she ever entered she had done so through a wipe. She wasn't sure it was safe to open a window.

She hadn't thought about it before, she'd always glanced at her mother's window box through the closed window while they sat and chatted in the living room. It had never crossed her mind that her mother must have opened her window to tend to the plants.

Her mother hadn't died... At least, she had died, but not because of the fresh air. Maybe the wipe at the entrance to her building and the one attached to her bathroom were enough to keep her safe. After all, Dharma had spent a couple of hours outside today, and she was fine.

Suddenly, she felt paranoid. What if she wasn't fine?

When she got back to her apartment building, Dharma took a moment to relax in the wipe, still holding the geraniums. She stepped into the lobby, waited for a moment, and then stepped back into the wipe and outside again. She breathed the clean air for a minute and then walked through the wipe one last time before climbing the stairs to her apartment. She needed the bathroom, and was more than happy to stand in its tiny wipe. Then she showered, and when she finally felt clean she changed into pyjamas and went back to look again at Charity Mott's marriage certificate.

There were ways to find out more, and on Monday that's exactly what Dharma would do.

Twenty-seven

"Tuesday," said Pax, marching into his bedroom, where Verity was standing on the ottoman, wearing his wife's wedding dress, while Faith was fussing with pins.

"We're going to get rid of the frilly shoulders and lose an underskirt," said Faith, "but it's quite a classic dress, so it'll look modern enough by the time I've finished with it."

"Honestly, Mum, it's lovely," said Verity. "I'm just glad it's not too tight on the waist."

"It's an Empire line. Hides a multitude of sins."

"Very appropriate," said Verity, "since this baby is born of sin."

"Not the time for sarcasm."

"Sorry, Mum. I kinda meant it as a joke."

"Nobody cares, these days, whether babies are born in or out of wedlock, or whether they have two parents and what gender those parents are. A family's a family."

"Easy for you to say when you have a conventional family."

"There's nothing conventional about you lot," said Pa.

Faith turned to her husband.

"Did you say something about Tuesday?" she asked.

"No, no… You carry on. I'm only sorting out a wedding, that's all."

"My sarcasm's catching," said Verity. "Not sure it suits you, though, Pa."

"Tuesday?" asked Faith.

"The wedding is fixed for Tuesday. I finally got a date, and it's perfect," said Pax. "The rations come in on Sunday, so even if we starve for the rest of the week, I figure it's worth it to have a decent wedding breakfast."

"I saved the butter and sugar from the last couple of ration drops, so I've got enough to bake a nice cake," said Faith.

"So what have you been putting in my tea?" asked Pax.

"I haven't been putting sugar in your tea for weeks. I've weaned us all of it, a bit at a time."

Pax patted his stomach. "I thought it was the rations making me thin. I didn't know you were plotting against me."

"Do you miss it?" asked Faith.

Pax thought for a moment.

"I can't say I do."

"Well, there you have it, then."

"Tuesday, Pa?" said Verity, stepping off the ottoman. "The Tuesday that's in five days' time?"

"That would be Tuesday 24th of June. Yes."

"Can you finish the alterations on the dress, and take in Pa's suit for Sage, by then?" asked Verity.

"I've already done most of it," said Faith. "I figured his size wasn't going to change much in six weeks. As long as Sage takes care of the garden for me, there's plenty of time. I can even alter one of my old posh frocks for a bridesmaid's dress for Charity, if you want."

"Do you think she'd like that?" asked Verity. "She's been different lately, more worried, and she's spending a lot of time in her room. I think she's got a bit of cabin fever."

"It'll cheer her up," said Pa. He stepped out onto the landing, and called Charity's name.

"What is it, Pa?" Charity asked from behind her box room door.

"Can we borrow you for a minute?"

A few seconds later Charity came out of her room and closed the door.

"Your mother wants you," said Pax, heading downstairs.

"Mum?" said Charity, putting her head around the bedroom door.

"Come and have a look through my posh frocks, and choose something to wear for the wedding."

"You can be my bridesmaid," said Verity.

"Can I wear the green one with the halter?" asked Charity.

"I–" Faith started to say something, but Verity cut her off.

"You'd look great in that. And Mum can alter it, if it's too big."

Charity went to rummage in the wardrobe.

"You know green's unlucky at weddings?" Faith whispered to Verity.

"Only if you're superstitious," Verity whispered back, "which I definitely am not."

"Have you found it?" Faith asked Charity. "Pop it on, and let's have a look at you."

"Are you sure?" she whispered to Verity.

"It turns out my sister isn't a brat, and life isn't going to be easy for her with a baby in this house. If it cheers her up, it'll be lucky for all of us."

"What are you talking about?" asked Charity, walking up to them in a dark green, silk dress, cut on the bias.

"We were just saying how good you'd look in that dress," said Faith. "We were right. It's perfect. That bias cut skims your body beautifully."

"It's too long, though," said Charity.

"That's because you're thinner than I was when I bought it. I'll take it up for you."

"Won't that mean you can't wear it again?" asked Charity.

"It's yours, now. You look better in it than I ever did."

"Thanks, Mum," said Charity, grinning. She lifted the skirt, so she didn't trip over it, and twirled in the dress.

"Prettiest bridesmaid, ever," said Verity.

"You just can't help being sarcastic, can you, V?" said Charity.

"No," said Verity. "I mean it... Not as pretty as the bride, but very pretty for a bridesmaid."

"The pregnant bride," said Charity.

There was more banter as Verity slipped carefully out of the wedding dress, so she wouldn't catch herself on any of the pins. Charity stepped up onto the ottoman, and Faith went back to work.

"You might want to tell your husband-to-be that you have a wedding date," said Faith. "And tell him he can come up in ten minutes so that I can have a look at him in that jacket."

"Thanks, Mum," said Verity, kissing her mother on the cheek as she left the bedroom.

"Looks like she's over the sarky phase," said Charity.

"We live in hope," said Faith.

116

Verity went out into the garden, where Sage was busy tending the veg patch.

"You're going to marry me on Tuesday," she said.

"Am I?" said Sage. "I'm looking forward to it already."

"Me, too," said Verity, putting her arms around his neck and kissing him. "Mum wants you to go up in ten minutes so you can try on that jacket. I think she's already made some alterations, and taken the trousers in. You're going to look gorgeous."

"No," said Sage, "you're going to look gorgeous."

"I suspect the truth is that Charity's going to look better than either of us."

"Not possible," said Sage. "You're radiant."

Verity swatted him on the chest.

"What was that for? Can't a man pay his bride a compliment?"

"That's what you say to pregnant women," said Verity. "Radiant."

Sage touched Verity's belly, which had grown over the past couple of months.

"Well begging your swollen belly's pardon, but you really are pregnant now."

"If it hadn't taken the registry office so long to sort itself, I wouldn't look like this. They said six weeks, and it's been a lot longer than that. Besides, pregnancy is a binary state. I'm just as pregnant as I ever was. There's no such thing as a little bit pregnant."

"Well, now you've got the bump to prove it," said Sage.

"Ugh!" said Verity.

"And the tits."

"Better. Except not better, because now you're objectifying me."

"You say that as if you've never objectified me."

"That's different."

"Okay," said Sage. "I'll stop objectifying you."

"Don't you dare. My emotional state's fragile right now, so all positive reinforcement is *good* positive reinforcement."

"You just let me know when you've decided on the rules," said Sage, kissing her.

"And you just go upstairs and get that jacket fitted. See if Mum can do something about the lapels… They're very 2020."

"I'm not taking on Faith," said Sage as he walked away. "If you want the lapels altered, you're going to have to talk to her yourself."

"Are you afraid of my mother?" asked Verity, laughing.

"I'm afraid of all the Mott women, and with good reason."

"Then it's a good job I'm going to be a Tuke, as of next Tuesday," said Verity.

Sage turned back to his fiancée. "You're going to take my name? I wasn't expecting that." He started to walk back towards her, and Verity met him halfway.

"I want us all to have the same name," said Verity. "You, me, and baby… All Tukes."

"Thank you. I love that. I love you." He kissed her again.

"Love you back, oh wise one," said Verity. "Now, go and get that bloody jacket sorted out before Mum starts shouting out of the window and getting all the neighbours het-up."

"Absolutely," said Sage, turning away, and walking back into the house, only stopping to take off Pax's wellies.

Verity watched him open the back door into the house, his jeans tucked into his over-socks, and smiled.

Twenty-eight

+The wedding's finally happening next Tuesday+

+That's great+

+Mum's given me her green silk dress. It's gorgeous. I wish you could see me in it+

+I will see you in it one day+

+Are you sure of that?+

+Today's a good day, all round... We got our latest test results this morning+

+And it's good?+

+I'm not contagious any more, and the rash has gone+

+You're immune!+

+That's what the test results say+

+That's brilliant... That's SO BRILLIANT!+

+There's no need to shout. LOL. We always knew I was going to be fine+

+I didn't always know that+

+It's you, you know... You've kept me going+

+You mean, the sex has kept you going+

+Well, I'm sure it hasn't done me any harm. LOL... It's all you, though, Chaz. I could never have got through this without you+

+Glad I could help... Frankly, I couldn't have got through all the happiness in this house without you. If I didn't have you to talk to, I'd feel like a spare wheel all the time... I do feel like a spare wheel+

+It's good, though, Charity. It's a new life+

+In a three-bed with five adults already living in it... And I feel guilty+

+What is there to feel guilty about?+

+Pa was talking about getting our old cot out of the attic, soon... I don't know why they kept it, it hasn't been used since I was a baby+

+I bet they're glad they've got it, though. It's a good thing+

+The problem is, Pa's working out where he can make a space to put it in Verity and Sage's room. He's talking about moving in there with Mum, because their room's bigger+

+You're dad's really into it, isn't he?+

+He's always been pretty organised, and he's hardly working at all. He was doing a lot when this thing started, even when he was working from home, keeping up with ordering and stock checking, and all that sort of stuff. He doesn't have anything to do any more. I guess the wedding and the baby are keeping him busy+

+Well, isn't that good?+

+I don't think him and Mum should have to change bedrooms, though. They've been in there for as long as I can remember. It doesn't seem fair+

+But they need space for the baby+

+If I wasn't here, they could use my room as a nursery... It would've been much simpler if I'd just died when I got this thing. Now, they're never getting rid of me+

+Don't say that, Charity... Don't ever say that+

+Spare wheel... Huge burden... That's me+

+Shut up, Charity, you don't know how lucky you are+

There was a short pause.

+What's going on, Abe?+

Silence

+How's your dad doing?+

+Not great... His viral load has gone through the roof+

+But, the new medication's been keeping him stable for weeks... I thought he was better+

+He was, but he's gone downhill fast in the past couple of days+

+Why didn't you tell me?+

+I was hoping it was just a blip... Hoping that his viral load would be down again this time... It's not... It's way up+

+So what are they going to try next?+

+Nothing+

+Abe... There has to be something! They can't just...+

+He's going to die, Charity. My dad's going to die, and I don't know how I'm going to handle it+

+Oh, Abe, I'm so, SO sorry!+

+Thanks, Charity... Sorry I snapped at you+

+I deserved it. Snap at me all you want... I'll be right here, all the way through this. I won't leave your side... I promise+

+You don't have to do that, Chaz... I don't know how long it's going to be, or what it's going to be like... I don't know what to think or what to do+

+Look after yourself, and be with your dad, and remember that I'm right here... That's all you can do+

+Thanks, Chaz... I'm dreading it... I'm dreading him going... I'm dreading the hazmats coming in to take him away... I'm dreading him not being here+

+I'll come... I'll find a way to get to you... We'll go through this together+

+I can't let you do that, Charity. They'll put you in prison... People die in prison+

+I'd go to prison for you... Besides, I'm immune+

+Don't joke about it, Chaz... Please, PLEASE, stay where you are+

+Okay... but I'm right here... And, we're going to talk about this again+

+As long as it's just talk... If I lost you, I don't think I could go on+

There was a pause. Charity filled it, suspecting Abe couldn't think what to text and imagining him sitting there in tears.

Charity texted to him until he was finally able to text back.

+I'm okay now. You're my lifesaver, Charity Mott... I'm going to go and be with Dad now+

+You do that... Take food and drink in with you... It'll be exhausting, and you need to be strong+

+I promise+

+I love you, Able Dole, and I'm right here, if you need me+

+I love you, too, Charity+

Twenty-nine

"What's that child been up to all weekend?" asked Pax, as he sat drinking tea with Verity.

"She's got a friend she talks to a lot," said Verity. "Maybe they're just spending some time together."

"She hasn't even eaten with us. She takes her food to her room... And never brings the dirty plates back down."

"Do you want me to have a word with her, Pa?"

"I just want everyone to be happy," said Pax. "I worry that my baby girl isn't happy."

"It's hard to be happy in the Deluge," said Verity.

"You seem to manage it,"

"Charity hasn't got a man, she isn't pregnant, and she's not getting married. I've got a lot to be happy about, and a lot to be grateful for... Including you, Pa."

"Charity's got us," said Pa. "She's going to be a bridesmaid and an auntie."

"Trust me, when you're a teenager, that isn't the same thing at all."

"This friend?" asked Pax.

"That's her business. She's an adult. She's proven that over the past few months. She's about to turn eighteen, but she's older than her years. She had to grow up far too soon and far too quickly. She never got to do what the rest of us did when we were her age."

"You're probably right."

"Let her have her friend," said Verity. "And what does it matter if it's a boy? He's probably a very nice boy, and it's not as if he can hurt her, or get her pregnant."

"You're wrong, there. He can definitely hurt her emotionally. I don't want to watch my child going through a heartbreak."

"We all get our hearts broken," said Verity. "It's part of growing up, a rite of passage, even. Charity's got a good head on her shoulders, and she's found someone outside of these four walls that she can relate to. That's got to be a good thing... Right?"

"Yes, of course," said Pax. "You're right. And, not for nothing, you've grown up an awful lot too. A year ago I would never have expected you to be the wonderful woman you've become."

"I'll take that as a compliment," said Verity, laughing, "although, it makes me wonder what kind of a woman you did expect me to grow into."

"Oh I knew you'd be wonderful. I just didn't know you'd be so wonderful so soon."

Verity gave her father a hug.

"My oldest daughter's getting married the day after tomorrow," said Pax. "It hardly seems possible... Do you think your sister will have reappeared by then?"

"I don't think she'd miss wearing that dress, or seeing a new face, even if it is only a registrar on Zoom... not for the world."

"I hope you're right."

"Right about what?" asked Faith as she walked into the sitting room.

"I'm a grown woman and I'm going to be a mother, I'm pretty sure that guarantees I'm going to be right about everything from now on," said Verity.

"Not all the while you're living under my roof," said Faith, smiling. "I got here first. Now, come and try on this dress."

"You've finished the alterations?"

"I think so. I just want one last fitting to make sure, and promise me you won't get any bigger between now and Tuesday."

"Pretty sure I can manage that," said Verity, following her mother up the stairs.

"Charity," Faith called, as they reached the landing. "Do you want to come and see Verity's dress?"

"I'll see it on Tuesday," said Charity, loudly enough for them to hear her from behind the closed box room door.

"Do you think she's okay?" Faith asked as they stepped into her bedroom.

"I just had a chat with Pa about her," said Verity. "Yeah. It's hard for her, but I think she's doing okay. She's been texting someone quite a lot the past few months."

"A boy?" asked Faith.

"Yes, Mum, a boy. It's not a bad thing, you know."

"I never said it was. The little bastard had just better not die before this is all over."

"Mum!" said Verity.

"Sorry, but we all know that a lot of people are dying. I don't want Charity to have to grieve her first love. I know she's almost eighteen, and I know that the Deluge has forced her to grow up and face reality... This is just one reality I don't want her to face yet."

Verity put her arms around her mother. "It's all right, Mum," she said.

Faith brushed tears from her cheeks, and pulled herself together.

"Right. Get that dress on, and let's see how you look in it. I got the veil out of its box, too, if you want it."

"Thanks, Mum. I don't think I want to cover my face. I want to be right there when this wedding happens. I want to experience every moment of it, face-to-face with Sage, and with you lot, too."

"Good choice," said Faith. "Besides, it might be a little over the top for a Deluge wedding."

"My Deluge shot-gun wedding," said Verity, smiling. "That's going to be a tale to tell the baby."

Faith smiled back.

"I'm going to be a terrible mother, aren't I, Mum?"

"You're going to be the best. Anyway, it doesn't matter how hard you try, you can't keep your own truth from your kids. They see right through you."

Thirty

+He's gone, Chaz+

+Oh, Abe, I'm so sorry+

+No... It's okay. It was calm in the end, easy. He told me he loved me, and then he just wasn't there any more+

+Still... I'm sorry+

+He looks like he's asleep... Do you think I should cover his face or something?+

+Do you want to?+

+No... He just looks like he's a sleep. If I do, he'll really be dead+

+If you don't want to cover him, you shouldn't+

+I want to sit with him for a bit+

+Do you want me to go?+

+No, stay with me... Can you stay with me, Chaz?+

+I'm right here+

+Should I let them know, so they can pick him up?+

+Do you want to?+

+I just want to sit with him for a while+

+Do that, then. You can let them know when you're ready. It won't make any difference+

Charity hoped that she was saying the right things. It was sad, but talking to Able felt natural at least.

+Do you think?+

+Yes. Sit with him for a while+

+Stay here, though, Charity... Don't leave me alone+

+I won't... I'm right here+

Charity sat in silence, waiting for another text from Able. She thought that she could imagine him, sitting at his father's bedside. She could see him clearly in her mind, as the boy she'd been at school with. She didn't know what his father's room looked like, never having even set foot in the house. She didn't know what the bed was like, or the bed linen. She didn't know if the room was carpeted, or whether the curtains were open or closed. She didn't know what the furniture in the room was like, or how big the room was. She didn't know whether Able was sitting on the bed with his father, or whether there was a chair he could sit in. She didn't know whether the door was open or closed, or whether there were any lights on.

Charity thought about all of these things. She wondered whether Able was crying, or whether he was talking to his father. She wondered if the room was silent, or whether Able had left a television or radio on, for the comfort, for the company.

She could picture Abe's face, but she'd never seen his father.

She thought about what it would be like sitting, watching her own father die, and couldn't imagine it. She felt more lonely than she had ever felt in her entire life, and she knew that Abe must be feeling infinitely more lonely than she was.

Able had known the end was coming, and they'd been texting, more-or-less nonstop for two days. She knew that he hadn't slept, and she wondered whether he'd eaten, or if he'd only left his father's side to take a pee every so often. She hoped he'd at least kept himself hydrated.

She didn't know anything.

The Deluge had taken so many people. A lot of old people, but younger ones too. Charity hadn't been close to her grandparents in Leeds but she'd seen how Pa was when they'd died, during the first phase of the pandemic. They were old, and he claimed that it wasn't a tragedy, but it had made him so insistent that he'd wanted Verity at home with them, and he'd made that happen.

Maybe that's what grief did. Maybe it made you cling tighter to the people you loved.

Charity loved Able, and Able loved Charity. He had nobody. His mother had left when he was a toddler, and he'd never seen her since. He didn't know where she was, or whether she was alive. His father had worked hard, often for long hours, so Able had been in a lot of after school clubs and holiday clubs. He was a geek. He loved movies and games, and he was good at school. He even read books, voluntarily. But Charity knew that the man she loved wasn't a loner… He was just lonely.

He didn't have to be lonely. He had her.

+I think I'm going to let them know, now+

+If you're ready, Able. There's no rush+

+I'm ready. I don't want to cover his face up, though+

+That's okay. They'll do it+

+I'm going to say one last goodbye+

+Yes+

+Then I think I'll shut his door, and wait downstairs for them+

+That sounds good+

+I don't want to see him go… He wouldn't want me to see him go, not like that+

+Of course. Let them do their job+

+He's gone now, anyway+

+Yes, Able… He's gone… But I'm still here+

+Wait for me to text you back. I'm going to let them know+

+I'll be right here. I love you Able+

Tears were streaming down Charity's face. She would have given anything for Able not to have to go through all of this alone. She kept her line open, so that she'd be there when he needed her. There was nothing else she could do. She didn't know how long it would be. It might be hours, maybe days… Surely not days! It could be hours. She'd wait for as long as he needed. He'd text when he was ready.

Charity lay down on her bed, in silence. Her mother called up to ask her if she wanted a cup of tea. She shouted that she didn't. Some time passed, and there was another call for something to eat. She shouted, "No thanks."

Shortly afterwards, there was a knock at her door.

"I've left you a tray on the landing," said her mother.

"Thanks, Mum," she called back from behind the closed door. She tried to sound cheerful, because it was only a couple of days until the wedding and she didn't want to be a killjoy. It was difficult. She was tense and sad, and she couldn't do anything until she heard from Able.

+He's gone, Chaz. They've taken him away+

+Are you okay?+

+I didn't see him go… He wouldn't have wanted me to see him go, like that+

+You did the right thing+

+I don't know how to feel+

+I think that's normal, Abe. I think it'll be okay+

+Dad wanted me to live a good life+

+Of course he did+

+He told me so… He knew that I was going to be okay… That I'm immune, now… I think that's what kept him going+

+Maybe+

+I've got to live a good life, Charity, and I want to live it with you+

+I know, Able. You will! You're clever and funny, and loving. We'll have a good life together+

+One day+

+Now, Able. We shouldn't waste time, and you can't be on your own… We have to have a good life together now+

+It's what I want, but I can't ask you to do that, Chaz+

+I asked you+

+It's dangerous+

+Not for us… We're immune, remember+

+The guards+

+Do you want me there or not, Able? Because I want to be there+

+More than anything in the world right now+

+Leave it to me… Get some sleep, and eat something, and leave all the rest to me+

+I don't know, Chaz+

+I know… I know everything now+

Thirty-one

When Dharma returned to her cubicle on Monday she had lots of new internet searches lined up in her head. She was nearing the end of her current work project, and decided to finish it before she took her break.

At half-past-two, Dharma sent her report to head office and switched to her internet connection.

"Statistics: Marriages during the Deluge," she said.

+Additional data+

"Statistics: Registered marriages 2040 to 2043. Graphic."

A moment later a graph appeared on Dharma's screen. It was a simple diagram, showing number of marriages on the y axis and quarters of the years on the x axis. The graph showed a line that wove its way steadily upwards before dropping off slightly, early in 2043, and then plateauing, still at a higher than average rate, for the remainder of the year.

Dharma was learning that people had needed each other during the Deluge. Death did strange things to their relationships. They sought each other out, and coupled-up more readily during the pandemic. She had assumed that the incidence of marriages would go down, since people were dying in their thousands, but she was proven wrong.

"Statistics: Average age at registered marriage 2040 to 2043. Graphic."

Another graph appeared on the screen. The y axis recorded average age, and the x axis was divided up, as before, into quarters of the year.

In 2040, before the Deluge, the average age at marriage was twenty-nine. It was less than ten years after most people in the New Wave would finish their educations and leave their mothers, but it didn't seem totally unreasonable to Dharma. They were different times.

By the end of the period, the average age to get married had dropped to twenty years and eight months.

Dharma knew that most people under twenty-five had survived the Deluge. It had hit the over 60s the hardest, and had made a huge impact on the mid-life generation in their 40s and 50s. Many of the people in that age bracket had died as a result of contracting the Deluge virus while doing essential work to keep people fed, and to ensure essential services. The medical profession had been hardest hit in the 40 to 60 age group, where death rates had been second only to those in the over 60s.

Perhaps that was part of it. People were losing their parents younger, so were building new families to compensate.

Dharma was guessing. She was good with statistics and she was a good data analyst, but discerning the emotional or psychological reasons for people's actions was incredibly difficult and often counter-intuitive.

Verity had been about the average age for people marrying in the second and third quarter of 2042. Charity had married younger than the average in 2043, but not outside the statistical range.

Dharma looked for graphs of birthrates for the same period and was again surprised. More babies were born, as a percentage of the general population, during the Deluge and for two years afterwards.

It was hard to have and to raise a child. In the New Wave it was an intensely isolating experience, mothers considered extraordinary. They were paid to have and to raise a child. It was their whole life, their whole World. It was one of the reasons she wasn't ready to have a child of her own. Dharma had been the only witness to her own mother's life, and didn't want that for herself.

She looked at more statistics. The average age of first time mothers plummeted during and directly after the Deluge. It was even lower than the average age of people marrying.

She quickly realised that Constance had been born only three months after Verity and Sage were married. She knew that human gestation took thirty-nine weeks, from the science school downloads she'd read. She speculated that people had a lot of sex during times of crisis, and the bigger the crisis, and the higher the death toll, the more sex they had. The result was that more babies were born during those periods, many of them outside of marriage.

Dharma thought back to her history lessons about the Second World War and tried more internet searches. It was harder to find reliable data, because she already knew that record keeping relied on the population to register births, deaths and marriages. It was also a very, very long time ago, so most of the data would be obsolete and therefore expunged from the internet. Dharma pieced together the few bits of data that she was able to find, and her theory appeared to be borne out.

People married younger during the World War than they did for the rest of the twentieth century. They had children younger, and many of those children were not born inside marriages.

It had to be about crises, and it had to be about basic human needs during difficult times. During the war, people had formed relationships and had children, and the same thing had happened during the Deluge.

Dharma was now convinced that the registration of marriage that she had found for Charity Mott was genuine, and that her great-aunt was not so unusual at the time, for marrying very young. The record was of the old type, before the New Wave records were established. Dharma wondered whether there was any chance she might find a birth associated with Charity and Able Dole. It was a long shot, but it didn't seem impossible.

Dharma liked a long shot. She liked the outliers in the statistics that she analysed on a daily basis.

"Birth register for Able Valor Dole, father, and Charity Grace Dole, formerly Mott, mother," she said into the VR.

+Data not found. Complete *Field+

"Show Field."

She looked at the screen. "Lewisham," she said, confidently. She knew that no one had been allowed to move around during and after the Deluge. Most people were on lockdown for months. Some of the restrictions had finally been lifted after the pandemic had burned itself out, but, by then, many people had become used to a new lifestyle and had chosen not to move, even if they were eligible for relocation.

Dharma hoped that Charity and Able had stayed where they were.

Thirty-two

Pax had propped up the computer, so that they could all stand for the ceremony.

"Nobody in their right mind gets married sitting down," he'd said. It had made Sage laugh. Charity was holding up a laptop, with a Zoom call to Sage's parents, who came online a moment after the main computer screen went live.

Sage laughed again when he realised that the registrar conducting the ceremony was sitting at what looked like her dining table, with a dresser of dishes behind her. At least they were attractive dishes, and Harmony Kimmel was neatly dressed in a smart shirt and business jacket.

"Oh, you all look lovely," she said, when the Zoom feed finally went live. "I've married people in their pyjamas before now. I won't feel over-dressed for this one. How glorious."

Charity popped out in front of the computer, partly to show the Tukes to the registrar and partly to show the registrar her dress.

"You look gorgeous, too," said Harmony Kimmel. "I don't often get to see a beautiful bridesmaid these days."

"She seems nice," Sage whispered to Verity, standing next to him and holding his hand.

Verity leaned in, and whispered back, "She could be in her knickers under that table for all we know."

They both laughed.

"I'm sorry," said Harmony Kimmel. "Is something the matter?"

"Nothing at all, Ms Kimmel. We're just happy. That's all."

"You can call me Harmony," said the registrar. "And I'm happy to be here, too. It all looks so lovely and festive!"

"Thank you, Harmony," said Pax, leaning slightly towards the screen, "but I think our time's limited, so perhaps we should get this wedding underway."

"Of course. Let's begin.

"We are here today to celebrate the marriage of Sage and Verity. On their behalf, I would like to welcome you all, and thank you for allowing me into your home to perform this celebration. I know it means a great deal to them that you are with them, in person and online, to share in their happiness on this wonderful occasion.

"Your home at 131 Engleheart Road, Catford, SE6 has been sanctioned according to interim laws for the celebration of this marriage. You are here to witness the joining in matrimony of Sage Valor Tuke and Verity Cornelia Mott. If any person present knows of any lawful impediment to this marriage, they should declare it now."

Pax glanced at Charity, who stuck her tongue out at him.

"I usually ask the bride and groom to stand at this point, but since you're all already standing, we can move on to the next bit.

"Before you are joined in matrimony, I must remind you of the solemn and binding character of the vows you are about to make, especially in these difficult times. Marriage, according to the law of the country is the union of two people, voluntarily entered into for life, to the exclusion of all others.

"The purpose of marriage is that you may always love, care for and support each other through all the joys and sorrows of life, and I can see that you already have a little joy on the way, but I digress…

"That love may be fulfilled in a relationship of permanent and continuing commitment. Today, Sage and Verity wish to affirm this commitment in the presence of their families, and offer each other the security that comes from legally binding vows, sincerely made and faithfully kept.

"Sage, please say the following words after me. 'I solemnly declare that I know of no lawful reason why I, Sage Valor Tuke, may not be joined in matrimony to Verity Cornelia Mott'."

Sage smiled, and said his vows without hesitation.

Verity looked very seriously at the screen when it came to her turn to respond.

"I solemnly declare that I know of no lawful reason why I, Verity Cornelia Tuke… I mean Mott, may not be joined in matrimony to Sage Valor Tuke."

"I see that you're taking his name," said Harmony. "That's lovely, since you're having the baby... Sorry, just a bit more.

"The moment has come for Sage and Verity to contract their marriage before you, their families. Do you have rings?"

"I have a ring for Verity," said Sage. "Thank you, Faith."

"Oh!" said Verity. "I didn't know. Thanks, Mum."

"It's the eternity ring your father bought me when you were born."

"Thank you, too, Pa," said Verity.

"We should probably get on with it," said Pax, beaming.

"You're so adorable," said Harmony. "Right, Sage, please say the following words after me. 'I give you this ring as a sign of our marriage, as a token of my love and affection, and as a symbol of our commitment to each other. I call upon our families to witness that I Sage take you Verity to be my lawful wedded wife. I promise to love and care for you, honour and respect you, and share everything I have with you. I look forward to our future together with hope and happiness, and I'll always remember the feelings we have for each other, today.'"

Sage cleared his throat, took Verity's hand, and put the ring on her finger. Still holding her hand, he repeated the words and then Verity immediately did the same.

"Good for you," said Harmony when Verity finished. "That was almost word-perfect, and I didn't have to read it out for you."

"Does it still count?" asked Verity.

"Totally. Now, Sage and Verity, you have both made the declarations prescribed by law, and you have made your promises to one another in the presence of your families. Let us hope that this day will form a special memory in your lives to look back on with much love and happiness.

"Sage and Verity, it gives me great pleasure to declare that you are now legally married."

Sage leaned down and kissed Verity. Pax and Charity cheered, and Faith clapped her hands.

The Tukes also waved and cheered, before their screen blinked out, the connection lost.

"Well," said Harmony. "This was really lovely. I'm glad I was able to perform your wedding. I'll remember it."

"Thanks, Harmony," said Sage, waving at the screen.

The Zoom meeting closed abruptly, the connection lost.

"Just in time," said Pax. "Now all we have to do is sign the online form, but I don't expect we need Ms Kimmel for that. He reached for the computer while everyone else embraced and kissed each other.

"Here you go," he said, offering the touchpad to Sage. Sage wrote on it with his finger, and an approximation of his signature appeared, more-or-less in the correct field on the screen.

"Now you," said Pax.

"You're really eager to get me married off, aren't you Pa?" said Verity, smiling as she signed her name on the touchpad.

"He's just hungry for cake," said Charity.

Verity looked at the screen. "Should I do it again? That looks nothing like my signature, and it's on the diagonal."

"It's done," said Pax. He added his signature as a witness.

"Your turn," he said, putting the touchpad in front of Charity.

"Me?".

"We thought our other witness should be our only bridesmaid," said Verity.

Charity blushed as she wrote her name on the touchpad.

Pax glanced at Charity's signature, sent the form, and then shut down the computer.

Verity kissed Sage, again.

"I'm glad your mum and dad could see this," she said. "I'm sorry you didn't get much time with them."

"It's all good. Mum will no doubt send me a long text about it later."

"And more cake for the rest of us," said Charity.

"That too," said Sage. "Now give me a hug, Sis."

"Only if you never call me 'Sis', ever again," said Charity, putting her arms around her brother-in-law.

She realised that she was holding him a little too tightly and for a little too long. She didn't care. She hugged Verity in the same way, and then both of her parents. They were good hugs.

"Cake!" said Pax, and they all went through to the kitchen, where Faith had laid on quite a feast.

"How long have we been going without so that you could hoard all this food?" asked Pax.

"Only since the engagement was announced," said Faith. "Hasn't my garden, sorry, Sage, our garden… Hasn't our garden fed you well enough?"

"It has," said Pax, kissing Faith. "It really has."

"We still want cake, though," said Charity "Cut the cake! Cut the cake!"

"Well, if you insist," said Sage.

Thirty-three

Con checked his connections as soon as Joy had left for her lunch break. She had a standing order at one of the local lunch bars and was always gone for the full forty minutes. Con assumed it was so that she'd have more people to complain to.

The morning had been very strange. Joy had been confused by the change in dynamic in the cubicle since she'd left a fortnight earlier. She'd tried to whisper something to Con a couple of times, but he wasn't taking the bait. He felt a little guilty, and he had asked her whether she'd enjoyed her holiday, but as usual nothing had been right for Joy. Con found it hard to listen to her complaining, let alone sympathise with her. He'd much rather be talking to Blythe.

He didn't really want Blythe to know that he was checking to find out whether Dharma had kept an open connection with him. Blythe wouldn't be able to e-mail Dharma, until she decided whether she was going to free up one of her connections. He didn't want to get Blythe's hopes up, if Dharma had disconnected from him, and he didn't want Blythe to know that he could still communicate with Dharma when she couldn't

It was a bit of a dilemma.

"Aren't you going out?" asked Blythe.

"I thought it'd be nicer to sit here with you while Joy's out for lunch. I'll get us some coffee in a minute. What are you up to?

"Mum was horrible over the weekend, because I hardly connected to her at all last week," said Blythe. "So I've got my connection open with her so that she can rant at me some more."

"I'd better leave you to it, then. Good luck."

"Thanks, Con. I'll get the coffee today."

Con was relieved. If the connection with Dharma was still live, he could send and receive e-mail without Blythe knowing anything about it, and he wouldn't have to lie about what he was doing because she was busy anyway.

Con's screen blinked, and the connection came to life. He was in communication with Dharma.

He didn't know what to say, or how to begin, so he started by telling her who he was, and his relationship to Blythe. He said they were friends, and that he was using some of his computer capacity to help her out, checking the data.

He didn't expect an answer until at least the following day, so he was surprised when real-time was enabled.

Con and Dharma talked about the data, back and forth, for about twenty minutes. Con was reassured that Dharma knew what she was doing, and Dharma was reassured that Con was rigorously checking the data.

+Does Catford mean anything to you, Concord?+

+Reference+

+Location+

+Sorry. Nothing+

+OK+

Concord was clearly a dead end. Dharma's mother remembered the name Bromley, but that didn't mean that other old, local names were still in use.

+Problem?+

+No problem. Must sign off. Bye, Concord+

The connection froze. The opportunity for realtime e-mail had been disabled by Dharma.

What was she thinking? Con got up and put on his sweater.

"I'm done," he said, as Blythe tapped away at her keyboard. "I'll get the coffees; you talk to your mum."

"Thanks," she said, without looking up from her screen.

Con got their coffees, all the while wondering why Dharma had cut him off so abruptly. He put Blythe's drink on her computer station. He glanced at her screen, which was full of text, some of it in all caps. Clearly Blythe's mother had reached fever pitch.

He sat down at his own station and looked at the last communication he'd had with Dharma. He wondered why she'd asked him about a location he didn't recognise, that wasn't a New Wave address, and why the answer had driven her away.

Catford, he thought to himself. *Catford... Catford...*

He took another sip of his coffee. If Dharma had asked him about Catford, she must have thought he might know it, so the answer must lie somewhere in the data. Dharma was all about data.

They'd exchanged almost no personal information, so why did she want to know about a location called Catford?

'Catford... Data...'

Con wasn't seeing it. There were still ten minutes remaining of his lunch break, and he didn't want to disturb Blythe while she was busy placating her mother. He pulled up the data sheets that Dharma had uploaded for him, and set a search parameter for Catford.

+Data not found+

He thought for a moment, and then reset the parameters.

+Catford. Closest match+

One of the data sheets cycled to the top on his screen. Con glanced at it, and then zoomed in. It was a birth certificate for Constance Tuke. There was an old address in one of the data fields, which had a red box around it. Con stared at it for several seconds.

+ 131 Engleheart Road, Catford, SE6+

He sat back again, his mind processing data, quickly and efficiently.

His office address was 159/RhGbCT/SEd6. The first three digits matched the first three digits in the old style address from the certificate, dated 2042, and with the addition of a lower case 'd', the end of the address matched. What if he could find a current address that began '131', and ended SEd6?

"Thanks for the coffee," said Blythe, hitting a key to close her connection to her mother. She wheeled her chair a little away from her station.

Con closed his own screen and turned his chair to face her.

"Are you okay?" he asked. "I hope your mum didn't give you too much of a hard time."

"I'm fine," said Blythe. "It's what she does. What about yours?"

"My mother?" asked Con. "We were never close. She didn't like me. She never really accepted me."

"But you were at home for a long time," said Blythe. "You're ninetieth percentile."

"I liked to download school. It's really all I ever did, seven days a week, fifty-two weeks a year."

"That can't be true," said Blythe. "That's not a childhood."

"My mother couldn't offer me a childhood. As I said, she didn't like me, and, if she had liked me, I don't know if she'd have been able to be a conventional mother, anyway."

"It sounds terrible. People like that shouldn't have a child."

"I suspect that most people like that don't have a child," said Con. "Anyway, by the time I was seventeen I was ninetieth percentile, and I was out of there."

"I didn't think anyone left home that young."

"I spent some time in juvenile housing with people who'd lost their mums. I was a lot better off than they were. I could work, so I could choose my own tariff."

"And you didn't make any friends there?" asked Blythe.

"If anything, they disliked me even more than my mother did. I was cleverer than them, I didn't have to download school and manage on my own, and I had a much higher standard of living. Besides, I was only there for a few months, allocated independent housing when I applied on my eighteenth birthday."

"And you've been alone ever since?" asked Blythe. "I'm not surprised you like company… Even Joy's."

The handle turned on the cubicle door.

"Talking of whom," Con mouthed to Blythe, and they both smiled as Joy walked in.

"What are you two plotting over?" asked Joy. "Things seem to have changed around here, since my so-called holiday, and I'm not sure I like it."

"You don't like much, though, do you, Joy?" asked Con, smiling at her as she hung up her jacket

"That's none of your business," said Joy, glaring at him. "I don't know what's turned you so nasty, Con."

"It's Concord," said Con.

"Whatever." Joy sat at her station, and barely spoke for the rest of the day.

Thirty-four

Dharma was surprised when she found two birth certificates with Able Dole and Charity Tuke's names on them. The search had been laborious.

Both were dated 22nd January 2044. She selected one and looked at the field for the informant. Able had registered the births on the 15th February 2044 at Lewisham registry office. His address was 86 Bargery Road, Catford SE6.

The certificate was for a boy called Zen Dole.

Dharma was disappointed. Her aunt had given birth to a boy, which meant there was no female line to follow.

She looked at the second certificate, but assumed that it was either an error, or a duplicate of some kind.

She scrutinised the document carefully, and all the information was the same. Able Dole had registered the birth on 15th February 2044, and his address was 86 Bargery Road. The child who had been registered was a girl called Liberty Dole.

Dharma switched back and forth between them, in wonder. At only twenty years old her aunt, Charity Dole, had given birth to twins, a boy and a girl.

She went back to look at the old maps of Catford in 2040. Engleheart Road and Bargery Road were close together, certainly within easy walking distance if the layout of the streets was similar to BRd1. She guessed that the house where the Motts and Tukes had lived was less than half a mile from where the Doles lived. The family had stayed close to each other.

Dharma was thrilled to have found her mother's cousins, and she was thrilled that one of them was a girl. If she could trace that child forward through time, she'd be able to find out whether, like her cousin, she had also had a child. That child would be the same generation as Dharma, and, at that point, it wouldn't matter whether it was a boy or a girl, because her search would be over.

Dharma hoped that the twins had survived in the difficult years after the Deluge, through all the necessary changes that had followed. She hoped their buildings had been fitted with wipes, or that they had been born with immunity. She was full of concern for her baby cousins, even though they'd been born almost eight decades earlier. They were only about a year younger than her mother. If they were alive, she hoped that she could find them. If they were dead, it might be more difficult.

"Liberty Dole, 22nd January 2044, Catford E6, all data," she said.

A series of documents appeared on Dharma's screen.

The top one was the birth certificate that Dharma had already scrutinised. The next was the census for 2045, listing Liberty as a one-year-old girl. The rest of the data tallied with everything that Dharma already knew. She was getting close.

The next document was an education completion certificate, but much of the information had been redacted: large, black blocks filling the screen where the information should have been. It was dated August 2069, which suggested that Liberty had completed a second degree. Dharma was pleased that the girl was clever. She would have been twenty-five when she started work.

Next came a housing placement. It was a brief document, dated November 2069, and most of it had also been redacted, but it showed that Liberty had been allocated a place of her own.

Next, a company employment contract dated January 2070, right around Liberty's twenty-sixth birthday. Again, it had been heavily redacted. Next came an employment severance record, dated January 2080.

Liberty had completed her ten years of employment, so this would have been when she could have a child.

Dharma took a breath before moving on to the next record. She hoped that it would be a birth record, and that there might be enough information on it for her to go forward into her own generation. She uploaded the severance record to her home photo storage, and the screen blinked.

It was not what she was hoping for.

Dated November 2080, it was another company employment contract. Dharma wondered why Liberty had experienced a short period of unemployment. It was rare in the New Wave. Some people held the same positions in a company their entire lives; others were promoted or even demoted within the same company. She did not know of anyone who left employment for almost a year and then returned. She would have loved to know what was hidden beneath the black blocks that covered the document.

Dharma had uploaded each of the documents to her home photo storage. She hoped that her analytical brain might work out some through-line for Liberty Dole's life. She needed something if she was ever going to find the woman.

The next document was another employment severance record, dated December 2088. Liberty had terminated her employment in time for her forty-fifth birthday.

Dharma knew that this was the last realistic opportunity for Liberty to have a child. Dharma had been born in February '85, a few months after her mother's forty-second birthday. If Liberty had a child in 2089, it would be close to her own age.

She uploaded the document, holding out little hope for a birth certificate, but there were still files waiting to be examined.

The next was a housing placement dated July 2093. This confused Dharma, again, and she was disappointed that there was no birth certificate for 2089 or 2090.

The next document was dated October 2093.

It didn't seem possible. Liberty Dole was only three months shy of her fiftieth birthday. This couldn't be a birth certificate.

Dharma picked through the information that had not been blacked out, and it certainly seemed to show that Liberty Dole had given birth to a child. All of the child's details had been redacted. Nevertheless, this appeared to be a New Wave birth registration.

Dharma had a cousin. He or she would be approaching her twenty-seventh birthday.

Dharma sat, thinking about that for several minutes. She remembered being twenty-six, new to life in her own flat without her mother, new to the work that kept her busy all day and which she enjoyed so much, new to the luxury of a higher standard of living. She hoped that this cousin of hers was as optimistic and content, as she had been at twenty-six.

Liberty Dole would be about the same age that her mother had been when she'd died. There was a good chance that she was still alive, somewhere. Seniors had allocated housing, and were well taken care of. She'd seen it with her own mother. If she hadn't fallen in her bathroom wipe and hit her head, she'd probably still be alive. Her death had been sudden, and shocking, but at least Constance Tuke had been healthy and active before the accident.

Dharma double-checked that she hadn't missed anything, and that all the documents had been uploaded to her storage at home. There was no death record for Liberty Dole.

Dharma had to get back to work. She closed the screen and set about uploading the data she would be analysing over the next weeks or months. There was little for her to do, so she had plenty of time to think about her personal project while she checked and ordered the data uploads.

Thirty-five

The Motts and the Tukes spent the remainder of the wedding day talking and laughing, and eating the food that Faith had spent the previous night preparing. Pax even found a bottle of sparkling wine, so that they could toast the happy couple. Verity toasted with reconstituted orange juice, which sometimes came in frozen, cardboard tubes with the rations.

"It's nice to see so much of you for a change, Charity," said Pax, as they all sat around in the living room, relaxing. "What've you been up to the past few days?"

"Nothing much," said Charity. "I just didn't want to get roped into wedding preparations."

"There wasn't that much to do," said Faith.

"But if I'd been around, you would've found me something to do," said Charity, "and I didn't want to get behind with my school work. Pa might have forgotten about it over the past couple of months, but I knew he'd catch up with me again, as soon as the wedding was sorted. I didn't want to be behind."

"So, you've been catching up on homework?" asked Verity, some of her old, first trimester sarcasm creeping into her voice.

"Some."

"And Able?" asked Verity.

"He's fine, thank you very much. In fact, I might just go for a pee, and check in with him while I'm up there.

She got up from the sofa where she'd been sitting next to her mother, and left the room.

"Too much?" asked Verity.

"Just enough, I think," said Pax. "It's good that she knows we're aware of the boy. Gives her a chance to talk about him if she wants to."

"So, what you're saying is that you feel better about it, Pa?"

"You're just like your mother, Verity Mott," said Pax.

"Tuke," said Verity.

"Mott… Tuke… You're still the same Verity."

+The wedding's all done with. We're just sitting around, eating and drinking. I popped upstairs for a minute to say hi+

+Hi, Chaz. Hope you're having a good time. You should enjoy today+

+I'd enjoy it more if you were here with us… But, yeah, it's been nice. Everyone's happy, and it's a nice change from the usual day-to-day+

+I bet+

+Tell me how you are. What're you doing?+

+School, mostly… It keeps my mind off Dad. I wish he could've had a funeral+

+We'll give him a proper memorial service when this is over+

+Yeah… It's weird, though. I'm doing my schoolwork in the sitting room… I'm sitting in Dad's chair+

+That's nice+

+Yeah. It makes me feel closer to him, somehow+

+He's only been gone a couple of days. Things are bound to feel weird. Are you eating?+

+Yeah. There's more food in the house than I need for just me. I guess the rations will change next week+

+I guess so. Make the most of the extra food while you can+

+I'm not really hungry. I'm tired, though. I've been sleeping okay… I thought it might be hard to sleep+

+It's been an exhausting few months. Things will be better really soon. I promise+

+I hope so, Chaz+

+I promised, didn't I? And, I always keep my promises+

+You always do+

+Better go, or they'll start wondering what I'm up to+

+Enjoy your day, Chaz. It's good to think of you having fun+

+I'll try… Love you, Abe+

+Love you, too Chaz+

Charity wandered back into the living room, taking her time. She was expecting lots of questions about Abe that she didn't want to answer.

"Everything okay, kiddo?" asked Sage.

"All good," said Charity.

"In that case," said Pa. "I think I'll make a pot of tea. I'm sure we can all manage another slice of that delicious wedding cake."

"Tea would be lovely," said Verity. "Let's sit in the kitchen for a bit. If I stay here any longer, I'm going to go to sleep, and I want to make the most of my wedding day… I'm only going to have one."

"You bet you're only going to have one," said Sage, helping Verity up out of the low, soft sofa.

"Do you realise, we haven't done any gardening today?" asked Sage.

"Or any laundry," said Faith.

"We can all pitch in and catch up, tomorrow," said Pa. "Including you, Charity. You've been far too absent recently, been spending too much time in that tiny little room."

"Oh, leave her alone, Pax," said Faith. "Let her find her own way. She's doing her school work, and she seems stable and more-or-less content. That's good enough for me."

"Right you are. Gardening and laundry, and schoolwork, can all wait until tomorrow… We'll all pitch in, and get everything ship-shape in no time."

"I'm up for that," said Sage. "I love a bit of gardening. Never thought I would; never thought about it at all, until we came here. Maybe Verity can take it easy, though."

"I'm sure I'm capable of pottering about and doing a bit of tidying up," said Verity. "I'm not sick. I'm only pregnant."

"It's not hard to see who's going to be the boss in this marriage," said Pax.

"It wasn't hard to see who was the boss from the beginning," said Charity.

She was enjoying the company of her family, and this was a good day. In some ways she never wanted it to end, in other ways it couldn't end soon enough.

At about ten o'clock, Sage took Verity upstairs. She was exhausted, but she wouldn't let her new husband leave her side, even though they'd been in each other's company constantly for more than a year. She'd be asleep as soon as her head hit the pillow, but Sage was content to read a book for a while and then get a good night's sleep. He'd been working his way through Faith's extensive library of gardening books, and he'd been reading fiction from the shelves in the sitting room. Some were novels that Pax and Faith had collected over the years, some were from Verity' and Charity's years at school. Some were old and demanding, others more modern, and lightweight. There was even some science fiction, the early, classic stuff from the second half of the twentieth century. He'd loved the copy of Ursula Le Guin's *The Left Hand of Darkness* that he'd found on the shelf, and, alongside it, *Flowers for Algernon* by Daniel Keys.

Life was good. Science fiction made him hopeful that life could always be good, even during difficult times, even during the Deluge. It also made him feel hopeful that there could be a new life, a different life, after the Deluge. Perhaps there could be a better life for his child, in the future; Sage could think of no good reason why not.

Charity tidied the sitting room, and collected dishes, while Pax and Faith set to cleaning down and washing up.

"Why don't you go to bed now, too?" said Faith. "Your father and I can finish up here."

"Okay," said Charity. She kissed her parents on their cheeks and went back up to her box room.

"She seemed happy today," said Faith. "Affectionate, even."

"She'll settle," said Pax. "This whole thing has been a lot for a child to cope with."

"She's not really a child any more, though, is she?" said Faith. "We need to give her some credit… and some space."

"You're right," said Pax, "but I lost one daughter today. It'd be nice to keep Charity's childhood going for a little while longer."

Faith laughed. "Don't be so dramatic! We didn't lose a daughter today, and we're going to have a grandchild before much longer. We should let Charity find her own way, do her own thing at her own pace. Besides, she hasn't been a child in a long time… Not since the start of all this."

"Do you think it would have been worse if this had happened ten years ago, when they really were children?" asked Pax.

"Worse? Better? I don't know," said Faith. "I guess it would have been different."

Charity lay on the single bed in the box room, listening for sounds in the house. Verity was already snoring, softly. Sage was quiet, but Sage was always quiet.

She looked at her watch. It was a little after eleven-thirty. A few minutes later, she heard a bedroom door open, and Sage walk along the landing to the bathroom. A minute later she heard him walk back to his room. Charity thought she heard the light-switch being thrown, before Sage closed the bedroom door.

She was surprised how long it took her parents to go to bed. She waited for another hour before they came up the stairs, long after midnight. She wondered what they'd been talking about for so long in the kitchen. She knew that's why her mum had sent her to bed, so that they could have some private time to chat, and go over the day's events.

No one in the house had much time alone. Charity was lucky in that respect. She didn't blame her parents for wanting to spend that time together. Twenty minutes later, she heard her pa turn off the landing light, and close his bedroom door.

Charity felt ready, but she knew the timing was wrong.

When she was a child, Charity had run with the other kids, in the streets and down the many alleys that ran behind and between the older houses. She'd worked out a good route. She'd also sat up and listened every night for a week, her window open to the balmy June air. It was nice to feel the cool of the night, by contrast to the intense warmth of the days. The cool air had the added advantage of keeping her awake while she listened.

For the past week, she'd made a note of the times when she'd heard footfalls, or a cough or sneeze somewhere close to the house, and she'd kept a record of when the street lights went out, as dawn rose.

She still had a couple of hours to wait. At least.

At ten past the hour, every hour, give or take a minute or two, Charity heard someone outside. She even thought she heard someone peeing up against a wall at eight minutes past three.

The streetlights would start to fade out at four-thirty, and the sun would start to come up within ten minutes, so there'd be a crossover between the natural light, and the artificial.

Charity made her move at half past four. She'd decided not to take anything with her, except for her phone and id. The dress didn't have pockets, so she simply carried them. Taking the id was a risk; if she was stopped, the guards would immediately know who she was. On the other hand, her id entitled her to rations.

Charity needed to pee, but decided to wait. She didn't want to risk waking her parents. She tiptoed down the stairs to the kitchen, where she'd left her trainers by the back door that morning. Nobody had moved them. She picked up her trainers, and opened the door as quietly as she could. She wouldn't be able to lock it behind her, but that didn't matter; Pax would probably be up in a couple of hours, and crime had taken a dramatic downturn since the lockdown.

She closed the door behind her and walked down to the garden gate. She thought better of opening it, remembering that it squeaked, badly. Charity looked at the phone and id in her hand. She lifted her dress, and tucked them into the elastic in the back of her knickers. It had been a long time since she'd done it in gym class, at school, but Charity positioned her hands, and then raised a leg. Her gate-vault wasn't perfect, but it got her out of the garden and into the alley behind, and she was still on her feet.

Charity rubbed her hands together to get rid of the dust that had accumulated on the gate, retrieved her phone and id, and jogged down the alley. She stopped when she came to the exit onto Sangley Road, which she'd have to cross. She listened for a moment, hidden in the shadows at the mouth of the alley, and then darted across the road. Almost opposite, only three houses over, there was another back alley, but she decided to cut across the primary school grounds, instead. The guards would be patrolling the residential areas; they wouldn't bother with the school. Besides, there were no street lights on the school grounds, and she had good cover.

All she had to do was cross Culverley Road and it was back alleys all the way. She listened, her back against the wall that ran behind the school, and, hearing nothing, darted across the road. She didn't have to look out for traffic. No one had been allowed out at night for months, and during the lockdown nobody was using their cars. There were still a few vehicles on the roads: delivery trucks, ambulances and hazmat, but not at dawn.

Two minutes later, Charity was in the back alley of Bargery Road. She had to walk the entire length of the alley, so that she could start at the end house, number two, because the garden gates didn't have house numbers on them. She counted in twos, until she got to the gate that should belong to number 86.

She paused for a moment, hoping she was right. She thumbed the latch on the gate, and opened it, tentatively. People had given up locking their garden gates, and many left windows open and back doors unlocked. Charity was relieved that she didn't have to perform another gate vault, since the gate hinge had clearly been oiled regularly, and the gate opened almost without making a sound.

Once she was in the garden, the gate closed behind her, Charity looked down at herself in the green, silk dress, and wiped a little dust off it. She walked halfway across the lawn that covered most of the back garden, and then took off the trainers. They looked incongruous with the dress.

When Charity got to the back door of 86 Bargery Road she began by tapping, lightly. She didn't want to disturb anyone in the adjoining house, and she didn't want to be heard if there was a guard anywhere in the street nearby.

Charity didn't expect the first tap to be answered. She tapped again, but only slightly louder, expecting that she'd have to tap harder before she'd get an answer.

Almost immediately, a light was turned on in the kitchen, and she could hear someone moving around. Charity shifted a couple of steps to the left from the back door, to look through the kitchen window. She watched a figure, standing in the middle of the kitchen, blinking against the harsh, bright light. It rubbed its eyes.

When he had finished rubbing his eyes, and had adjusted to the light, Able looked around the kitchen. He thought he'd heard knocking, but perhaps it was his imagination.

Then he saw movement.

Charity was waving at Able from outside the kitchen window, trying to catch his attention.

His eyes turned towards her.

She waved again, just to be sure that he'd seen her.

Able stared.

Charity smiled.

Able stared some more.

Charity kept smiling.

Finally, Able broke into a wide smile, and then went out of sight as he rushed to the door. Charity stepped to the other side of the door, and listened to Able fumbling for the key, before, finally, pulling the door open.

"Come in," he said, through tears. "You're here!"

Thirty-six

Dharma scrutinised the New Wave documents the following lunch time. They were heavily redacted, but they were standard forms and, as a data analyst, Dharma had access to templates for all current registration documents.

It was a matter of a moment to bring up templates for work contracts and employment severance records, and for allocated housing. Dharma was familiar with the forms, since she'd had to fill most of them out at some time or another. She hadn't ever filled out an employment severance record, so she looked at that first.

Employment severance records were almost universally filled out by women for the purposes of having a child. There was a different form of record-keeping for retirees. The only other reasons for severance were employer requests to dispense with an employee, and most of those cases involved crime. Dharma knew this from some statistical analysis she'd done on white-collar crime, about eighteen months earlier. Her memories of it were particularly clear, because almost all of the crime had been trivial, but it had almost all been committed by men. Her data analysis was currently being used to implement changes in some forms of employment contract, to maintain productivity while limiting crime. It was a project she was particularly proud of, since it mostly dealt with the welfare of manual workers.

Dharma hesitated for a moment.

Most of her data analysis involved community and human behaviour. She had completed projects on juvenile delinquency, employee crime, senior well-being... The list went on and on. Sometimes, when new data came available, she completed more advanced analysis. She had been instrumental in alterations to school downloads and senior housing, as well as men in the workforce among other things.

She felt stupid. She had more access to more data than almost anyone, and she wasn't using it efficiently.

Dharma pulled up Liberty Dole's New Wave documents, and scrutinised them. Her original employment contract was heavily redacted, but, there, in the top right hand corner was her id number.

Dharma clapped her hands.

+Communication+

"Negative," said Dharma.

She shut down her internet connection, and logged back in on the W.W. intranet. It was monitored, of course, but the company would not know where she'd got the id number from, or who it related to. This search would be an outlier, but Dharma had made leaps of faith in some of her analysis that had sent her down similar paths in the past. This outlier should not register as a concern with the company. If it did, she could simply suggest that she might have misread the id number, and brush it off as a mistake.

Dharma's work record was impeccable, and she was a much-valued member of the team at W.W. She'd earned a number of incentives and bonuses, during her time with the company.

Dharma had memorised the number, since the sequence was very familiar to her, consisting of initials, birth year, parentage, and district code. She spoke the letters and numbers clearly into the VR.

Liberty Dole's education record was the first document to fill the screen. Dharma moved on to the next, and passed through several more, until she reached the first severance record, for 2080. Liberty Dole had left work in the hope of having a child, and yet she had returned to work within a year.

"Medical records," said Dharma.

The screen blinked, and the record began on the date of Liberty Dole's birth on the 22nd January 2044

"Scroll down, continuous." The document scrolled through at a little faster than reading speed, but Dharma got the gist of Liberty's childhood and early adulthood. "Pause," she said.

Dharma read the date for 2080. Liberty had become pregnant with a child, but had suffered a late miscarriage in her sixth month of pregnancy. She had returned to work only six weeks later.

Dharma had done data analysis for numbers of live births from sperm donation. Some of her work had been used to match donors with prospective mothers, but Liberty's miscarriage had happened forty years ago. The data was pretty basic then, and clearly Liberty had not found a good match. Her struggle moved Dharma, and she understood why the woman would want to return to work, and get on with her life.

"Scroll down, continuous," she said.

When the records reached 2088, Dharma paused again.

She read carefully through a number of pages. Liberty had been through a great deal to have her child. She had suffered a number of miscarriages, and undergone several minor procedures. Eventually, a diagnosis was made. Liberty Dole was producing antibodies that were dangerous to the sperm donations she was receiving. A sperm donor had been chosen, and the sperm had been processed and introduced directly to Liberty's eggs, which had been harvested. Liberty Dole had finally become pregnant, and given birth shortly before her fiftieth birthday. There was a note on her file that she was in the ninety-ninth percentile, by age, of women giving birth to live offspring.

"Scroll up." She had never heard of this kind of medical technology, and there must be a very particular reason why Liberty would be allowed to follow this course of action, or be subjected to it.

"Pause."

She was looking at the second contract of employment. Liberty Dole had worked as a genetic data technician at a sperm bank. She was responsible for one of the steps in the genetic matching of donors to recipients.

Dharma felt some surprise, but she liked the links that were forming through the generations of her family. Pax Mott had been a pharmacist, and Faith Mott had been a midwife. Their granddaughter, Liberty Mott, was in genetics, working with data, and she, Dharma was a data analyst.

Dharma could not help enjoying the evolution of her family's work, down the generations.

"Scroll down, continuous." She watched the pages go by for a few seconds, and then said, "Pause."

She looked at some data that showed Liberty Dole had been part of a fertility study run by the company that she had worked for. It explained why she'd had an extended period of unemployment before having her child.

A few moments later, Dharma was looking at the medical data for October 2093. October seemed to be a good month for births in her family. This child had been born on 11th October 2093, by caesarean section. She had been given a genetic code number within minutes of her birth at a facility in SEd6. That was unusual in the New Wave, and suggested that the child was at some risk. Codes were usually allocated when the child was released into its mother's permanent care, at five days old. A child couldn't be buried without an id number, and an id number couldn't be issued without a genetic code, so the codes were issued at birth to babies with health problems.

Dharma could hardly believe her luck. She already knew that there had been a child, a child who was now twenty-six years old, but she never expected to have access to her id number, and it would be easy enough to find Blythe's now that she had the genetic code. She found it, memorised it, and cleared her screen.

"BD1093CF1555/SEd6. All data," she said, into the VR.

All of the documents were New Wave, and some of them were partially redacted, but the first thing Dharma looked at was the name on the top left hand side of the screen, opposite the id number: Blythe Dole.

Dharma had a cousin, or a second-cousin, or a cousin-removed... She didn't know the exact relationship... But Dharma had a twenty-six year old cousin called Blythe Dole. Her birthday was 11th October 2093, and she lived and worked in SEd6. Her request connections code was easy. This was the New Wave, and one size fit all. Dharma hadn't needed to pull up Blythe's records to know her request connections code, because it was her id number. She just wanted to know something about her cousin, before she contacted her.

Dharma checked the time code at the top of the screen. She'd been looking at Blythe's data for 90 seconds, and she'd spent almost four minutes on checking Liberty's record. It was time to stop. She knew that the over-under on her record checks was in the three minute range, and she didn't want to raise any red flags with W.W. by stepping too far outside that range.

Blythe's id number was locked in her memory. It was one of those things that she would never forget.

Thirty-seven

"I said you'd get to see me in this dress." Charity was beaming.

"You told me I could trust you, and I can," said Able. "You do know what's best, and you do keep your promises."

"All true," said Charity, still beaming, her cheeks flushed.

They hadn't touched. They wanted to, but they didn't know where to begin, after months of texting each other. They hadn't even heard each other's voices.

"Your voice," said Able.

"What's wrong with it?" asked Charity, putting her hand up to cover her mouth.

"It's lovely," said Able. "It's lovely to hear it. It's deeper than I remember, more musical."

"Now you're just being silly," said Charity. "You sound just the way I imagined you would."

"And how is that?"

"I don't know. You just sound like you."

"Well that's good… I guess," said Able. "Why didn't we speak?"

"Texting was better. My house is pretty full and there's nowhere to go where I can't be overheard. Texting's more private."

"There's no one to overhear us now."

"Just us," said Charity.

"For how long?"

"What do you mean?"

"How long can you be here? When do you have to go home?"

"I am home," said Charity. "If you'll have me?"

Able almost rushed at Charity, putting his arms around her clumsily, and pushing too much weight against her. Charity braced herself, and leant into him to steady them both.

The embrace might have been clumsy, but it was warm and caring, and intense.

They stood together, like that, in the kitchen of his father's house, for what seemed like a long time. Able's head was close to Charity's, his neck bent so that he could rest it on her shoulder.

She realised very quickly that he was crying, silently. His body pulsed against her as he sobbed. All she could do was cling to him while he allowed his emotions to pour out. He cried for his father and for himself. He cried with grief and loneliness. Then he cried for the solace of being held, for the comfort. Then he cried for joy.

Charity realised that she was crying, too. She didn't weep or sob, but she shed a tear for her old life, and for her family. She knew that she'd miss being with them. Mostly, she cried for Able, and for all that he had been through, alone. She did not know what that felt like, and she hoped that she would never know.

When this was over, Able would be like Sage; they would be brothers. Pa and Mum would love him and look after him too, this man that she loved so much.

When Able was finally still, Charity loosened her grip and he stepped back a little. Charity smiled at him.

"You should wash your face," she said.

"I should. I should have a bath, too. I haven't had a bath since Dad... I've put on clean clothes, though," he reassured her... "Pyjamas, anyway."

"You don't have to explain. Go and run yourself a bath and I'll make some tea. I don't suppose you've got something I could wear?"

"T-shirts, sweats, jeans, take what you want out of the airing cupboard... Here," he said, taking her hand and leading her out of the kitchen and up the stairs. He opened a door on the landing.

"Wow!" said Charity. "This is incredibly organised."

"I got a bit obsessive about stuff while Dad was sick. Sorry."

"Don't apologise," said Charity, kissing him on the cheek. "Don't apologise for anything. Any coping strategy is a good coping strategy."

"Mr Frith," said Able. "I would never have believed a couple of days ago that I'd be standing here listening to you quote Mr Frith."

"I wonder if he's okay," said Charity.

"Whether he is or not, he'll clearly live on for decades... All those kids he taught, quoting him like that."

"He had some good ones, though, didn't he?"

"He had some great ones. I didn't understand some of them, not until the Deluge."

"I'm still not sure I understand some of them," said Charity. "This one seems good for now, though."

"That, and 'Keep on keeping on'."

There was a pause as Charity pulled a pair of jeans and a t-shirt out of the airing cupboard. She held them against her chest.

"That's the spare room," said Able, pointing to a closed door, along the corridor at the front of the house. "If I'd known you were coming, I would've sorted it out for you, but it's yours. You can change in there."

"I really need a pee, first. I didn't dare go before I left."

"It's all yours."

"Go and have your bath," said Charity, coming out of the bathroom. "I'm sure I can find my way around, and I'll make that tea."

"Yes... tea."

"Pa's a pharmacist," said Charity, "and the first thing he always reaches for is a cup of tea. That's before he gets out a thermometer or hands out the paracetamol. I don't suppose it cures grief, but it might help. Come and find me in the kitchen when you're done."

"Promise you'll be there," said Able. "I'm still half-convinced that I'm dreaming you."

"I'll tell you what, leave the bathroom door open, and I'll leave the kitchen door open, and we'll be able to hear each other."

She went into the spare room to change her clothes and run her fingers through her hair. It had been a long, eventful day. She hadn't slept, and she'd been wearing the silk dress for almost twenty-four hours. She hung it on a wire coat hanger found on the back of the door, the sort you used to get from the dry cleaners. She had to roll up the hems of the borrowed jeans, and she'd need a belt, but they were fine, and she liked the slightly oversized t-shirt with the band logo on the front. She'd have to go without underwear until she could sort something out. It didn't matter.

Nik Abnett

Then, she skipped down the stairs, listening to running water in the bathroom as she went. In the kitchen, she splashed water on her face, and washed her hands with the dish soap that stood beside the sink. Then she filled the kettle, and opened all the cupboard doors to find mugs, tea bags and sugar. There was even a teapot, and there was plenty of milk in the fridge.

By the time Able came downstairs in shorts and a t-shirt, Charity was on her second cup of tea.

"What should we do first?" asked Able.

"You look like you need some sleep, and I should really have a decent wash."

"I want to do something real with you," said Able.

"Okay," said Charity, smiling. "We can find something real to do… What's the time?"

Able pointed behind him at a clock on the kitchen wall. Charity glanced up at it.

"Let's drink our tea for ten more minutes, and just sit quietly, and at six o'clock, I'm going to ring Pa. Is that real enough for you?" She smiled.

"That's almost too real," said Able.

Thirty-eight

Dharma didn't upload any new data to her photo storage at home. She wasn't allowed to take work product home or do her analysis on the data anywhere except in her cubicle. It was all confidential stuff. This counted as work product, because she had accessed it using the W.W. intranet. It didn't matter. She understood what had happened to Liberty, and she had Blythe Dole's name and id number.

Tomorrow, Dharma would contact her cousin for the first time.

She thought about it a lot that night. She didn't know what to expect. It was one thing reaching out, but reaching out to a complete stranger was practically unheard of. She had never done it herself, and she didn't know anyone else who had. She thought about it a little longer, and realised how few people she knew.

She lived in an apartment block, and knew her neighbours by sight. She rarely spoke to any of them, unless it was a casual greeting if they crossed paths in the lobby. She worked in a large office, but stayed in her single cubicle for the entire length of the working day. Again, she knew some of the others who worked there by sight, mostly from her own floor. She waved at the concierge every day, but didn't even know his name.

The last new person that Dharma had met was Patience Opie, the gardener at her mother's senior housing. It had been nice, and perhaps she would go back some time, talk to her some more and maybe accept some seeds to grow in a window box. That safe smell of geraniums.

Dharma didn't know what to expect from Blythe Dole. She wondered how *she* would react if some stranger reached out to her via her connections. It had never happened.

She had intranet connections with other people who worked for W.W. She got messages from 'data collection' and from 'implementation', but all of that was work related, and she hadn't exchanged any personal information with any of her colleagues.

She had always had her mother, of course, at least until recently.

If someone reached out to her, she thought she'd want to connect out of curiosity. Her specialism was data analysis, and a relation would be a fount of new data. Blythe Dole might not feel that way about Dharma, though. Blythe might not work in data, or in anything related.

Blood, though… Blood was important.

Dharma knew that Blythe's mother was still alive, so they no doubt had a connection. Perhaps that would be enough for Blythe.

Dharma wondered what stories Liberty had told Blythe growing up. She wondered if Blythe remembered more of the old stories than she did and whether they'd been told some of the same stories.

None of it mattered. She would request a connection and then wait to see what happened. If she didn't get a reply, perhaps she'd try again, in three months, or six, or perhaps a year. They were both young, and there was plenty of time.

Dharma knew that she had no control over Blythe, or over what Blythe chose to do. The only control Dharma had was making the connection request in the first instance, and preparing an e-mail in the event that Blythe was curious enough to enable the connection.

So, that's what she did. On Saturday, Dharma spent the day preparing to introduce herself to Blythe and tell her about her search. She couldn't include everything, and she had to include some data to convince Blythe that she was genuine. She began to work through the documents in her photo storage.

On Sunday, Dharma jogged back to her mother's old place. Her id let her into the grounds, and she walked through the garden. There was nobody else around, so she picked some of the geraniums, and jogged back home. The last time she'd come it had been a Saturday, so perhaps Patience didn't work on Sundays.

Dharma decided that she liked the distance, the amount of time she'd spent in the fresh air. It scared her less this time that she had been outside for more than two hours, where the air wasn't tested or cycled, and where she had no opportunity to walk through a wipe.

When she got back to her building, she walked just once through the wipe into the lobby. Then she jogged up to her apartment, where she showered and changed. The geraniums went into a cup of water.

She had never had flowers in the apartment before. She put them in the middle of the table where she ate, and then adjusted their position so that the light fell on them, shining through the purple blue petals and showing how fragile they were.

The first geraniums she'd brought home hadn't lasted overnight. They'd been held too tightly for too long, and hadn't been put in water. She hoped she'd be able to look at these in the morning, during breakfast.

Tomorrow was going to be a big day for Dharma. Tomorrow she was going to get in touch with her cousin.

"Blythe Dole," she said. "Blythe Dole and Dharma Tuke." The names sounded good together.

Thirty-nine

Charity could hear the ringtone as she held her breath. It sounded too loud, and was going on for too long. She counted the rings, and for a split-second she thought he wasn't going to pick up.

"Hello, Charity," said Pa.

"Morning, Pa. Are you up? I hope I didn't wake you?"

"I was just thinking about going downstairs to make your mother a cup of tea…"

Charity waited through the pause. Pa was coming to a realisation.

"Charity," said Pa. "You could've just knocked on my door if you wanted to speak to me… It's early, but you can always knock."

"Sorry, Pa," said Charity. "I couldn't knock on your door."

"Why? What's the matter? Are you ill? What's wrong?"

"It's time for you to pop downstairs and make a cup of tea," said Charity. "You'll probably want to pee first, too. I'll ring you back in five minutes… I'm totally fine, Pa… Promise."

Charity hung up.

Pax didn't wait to pee; he went straight to Charity's room. He tapped once, opened the door and looked in.

"Faith!" he shouted.

Sage was on the landing, outside the box room door before Faith had pulled on a robe. "What's the matter, Pax?" he asked. "You sound…"

"Run down and check the rest of the house… The garden, too," said Pax. He was standing in the middle of Charity's empty room, still holding his phone in his right hand, his left clutching his head. He had no idea what the hell was going on.

Sage ran down the stairs and Faith walked along the landing. She saw that Charity's door was open and popped her head around it.

"Oh, Pax," she said. "What's all the fuss about?"

166

Sage shouted from the bottom of the stairs, "She's not down here."

Pax was shaking when he hit the button to dial Charity back.

Charity jumped when the phone rang.

"Do you want me to go?" asked Able, half-standing from his seat at the kitchen table.

"Don't you dare," said Charity. She took a deep breath, and answered the phone.

"Charity! Where are you?" Pa's voice was higher and louder than usual. He didn't sound angry, exactly, but he was clearly worried and upset.

"Pa, I'm fine. Honestly. I couldn't be better. Everything's all right, I promise you."

"Where the hell are you?" Pa's voice had lost none of its urgency.

"Your stuff is here, but you're nowhere to be found. This isn't a big house, Charity, so where have you gone? What have you done?"

"It's better this way," said Charity.

"I think I'll decide what's best. And what's best is that you tell me exactly where you are, right now… I wouldn't mind knowing the why of it, either."

"I'm with Able… You remember Able?" said Charity.

"The boy? How are you with the boy…? *Why* are you with the boy?"

"Able, Pa. His name's Able. I'm only a couple of streets away, and I'm safe… I promise I'm safe."

"How did you get out of the house? How did you get a couple of streets away? What are you talking about, Charity?"

"We've been talking for a long time, me and Able. We were at school together, and then we got to know each in the group chats, and one thing led to another. We've been together for months."

"How can you be together?" asked Pa. "You've been with us."

"I've been living with you," said Charity, "but I've been talking to Able. We love each other, Pa."

"That's no excuse… You need to be with us… You're a child."

167

"I'm not a child. You can't be a child and live through the Deluge... It grows you up," said Charity. "Pa, I have to be with Able. He doesn't have anyone else. They took his dad away on Sunday... Hazmat. His dad died, Pa, and he doesn't have anyone else. It was just the two of them, and now it's just me and Abe."

Pax sighed. "That's terrible," he said. "I'm sorry for the boy... I really am. He can be looked after... There are places he can be looked after."

"He's eighteen. He's an adult. He has to look after himself. They expected him to stay here, on his own, and look after himself. He needs me, Pa," said Charity, "and I need him."

"Your mother wants to speak to you,"

"Charity, darling, are you all right?"

"I'm fine, Mum. I'm with Abe."

"Yes, I heard some of it. I wish you were here with us, Able, too, if he needs to be."

"You've already got a houseful."

There was a pause on the line.

"Mum?" asked Charity.

"We didn't drive you away, did we?" asked Faith. "I'd hate that."

Charity could hear tears in her mother's voice.

"No, of course not. I love you... I love all of you. I just need to be with Abe. It means that Sage and Verity can have the box room for the baby. Pa can have a new project, setting up a nice nursery."

"You shouldn't have left, Charity," said Faith. "We'd have found room for the cot, for the baby."

"I know we would, but I'm where I need to be. You must understand that... Maybe not right now, but if you think about it, I know you'll understand."

"I just love you so much," said Faith, crying.

"It's your father," said Pax, a moment later.

"Hi, Pa," said Charity. "Look after Mum... She's upset."

Charity was crying too, tears running down her cheeks, but she was trying to sound cheerful. "Make yourselves a cup of tea. We can talk some more later. Honestly, Pa, I did the right thing... I did what you would have done. Love you."

Charity hung up again. She waited for a minute or two, looking at her phone, but it didn't ring. She put it on the table.

"Are you okay?" asked Able.

"Of course I'm okay, said Charity, wiping away her tears, and smiling. "I'm with you, aren't I?"

Able got up from the table and went to her. The embrace was less clumsy this time, gentler. He kissed the top of her head, and smelled her hair.

"I love you, Charity," he said.

"I love you too," said Charity, "and I love that I'm here."

Forty

"Are you getting coffee, today, or shall I?" asked Con.

"I'm pretty sure it's my turn," said Blythe. "I'll go now. Joy should be clear of the building."

"Okay."

A moment later, Blythe was out of the cubicle and Con could begin his search.

+Address search: 131 ending SEd6+

The screen showed only half-a-dozen matches. Con punched the air. He was fearful that there might be a lot more.

He ran his eyes down the list, clicked on one of the addresses to save it, and went back to Constance Tuke's birth certificate, with the address 131 Engleheart Road, Catford, SE6. He compared it to the saved address, which read 131/EgRcCT/SEd6. He didn't know what the lower case 'c' represented, nor the lower case 'd', but the rest seemed to correlate. It was a leap of faith, but Con believed he'd found the right place.

+Map of Catford in 2020+ he keyed in just as Blythe returned with coffee.

"What are you doing?" She asked.

"Geography."

"Another one of your strange interests?" asked Blythe. "Like your fascination with nineteenth century novels?"

"I've got a thing for old maps, right now," said Con. He wasn't lying. He'd hate to lie to Blythe. "All those years spent downloading school. I just can't help myself."

"Well, good luck with that. I've got to check in with Mum. I still don't know what to do about Dharma."

"You'll work it out," said Con. "At least you've started a relationship with her. She knows you've got limited computer access. I'm sure she'll be patient."

"Thanks, Concord. You're a pretty decent person, you know?"

"I did know, but it's nice to know you see it too. Now, speak to your mother, before she starts to wonder where you are."

Blythe sat at her station, and opened her connection to her mother. It was going to be a very long thirty-five minutes. Her mother still hadn't forgiven her for being so absent the previous week.

+Address: 159/RhGcCT/SEd6, closest match+

The screen blinked and faded out. Only after several seconds did the map reappear, zoomed in on a smaller area. Con could see several streets, with names written along them. He scanned for anything beginning with an R that also had one of the other letters in the name.

"Rushey Green," he said.

Blythe turned her chair to face him.

"Now you're just saying random words."

"I just thought it was an exciting place name."

"You're weird," said Blythe.

"Not the first time you've told me that," said Con, smiling.

If only she knew.

He opened his connection to Dharma.

+Catford… I think we live in Catford. I think my office address is 159 Rushey Green, Catford SE6. I believe the current address for 131 Engleheart Road, Catford is 131/EgRcCT/SEd6. Both addresses are in the same district. I could go and look at the location!+

+You really do understand data!+

Con hadn't expected an immediate reply, but was impressed that Dharma had opened up a real-time connection so that they could talk. He glanced over his shoulder, but Blythe was still busy with her mother.

+Ninetieth percentile. Like you. I can't account for the 'c' and the 'd' in the current addresses, but everything else matches+

+Give me a minute.+

Dharma left the connection to Con open, and went back to the old map of Bromley, where she'd begun her search. She knew her own district well, she'd jogged it often enough, and she knew that it was a built up area. She chose the centre of the grey mass that represented Bromley town on the old map, and moved her fingers up and down the streets until she was convinced that she knew where she was. She believed that her office was in Stockwell Close, on the old map; Its New Wave address was 022/SkCcBR/BRd1.

Dharma traced her walk home with her finger, following the streets. She lived in Harwood Avenue... She was sure of it. Her home address was 044/HrAcBR/BRd1.

+Right, Concord. My address works out, too. I've checked it against an old map. My office is in Stockwell Close, Bromley BR1: 022/SkCcBR/BRd1+

+Can you verify with a second address?+

+Already done... You and I think alike. My home address follows the same pattern, when I traced it on an old map+

+Can we verify by working out the 'c' and the 'd'?+

+Is your office in a built up area, Con? I wonder if the 'c' might be a variable, but it's in both of our addresses.+

+Yes. I'm right in the middle of the grey patch on my old map. The streets are old, and close together around here. The biggest local market is close, too. What about you?+

+Same... that 'c' connotes a built up area+

+Central? Or Centre... Could it mean urban centre?+

+Sounds plausible. What about the 'd' in the last portion? I'm 'd1', but you're d6+

+No idea. We've got four addresses that match up, though, five, if we include Engleheart Road+

+So the New Wave address system is a version of the old one... That should make it easy to find virtually anywhere!+

+That's crazy. Why didn't we know this?+

+We didn't need to know. We all stay where we are. We all live and work in the same place+

+It's the New Wave law+

Con thought about what he had typed, and realised that it wasn't strictly true. No one had to stay where they were. It was possible to move from one district to another, with permission. When that permission was granted, a travel route was authorised and transport provided. No one travelled very much, but that was mostly because travel had to be justified and authorised. Joy had once talked about her mother having to travel to her grandmother's funeral, across districts. The funeral had to be put on hold for almost a month, so that Joy's mother could fill out all the forms, get permission, and receive the route and transport details.

+Do you know where I am?+

+I think you're about six miles from where I am, Concord+

+That doesn't sound like very much+

+It isn't+

+?+

+I used to visit my mother every weekend, and jog the six miles there and back+

+Across districts?+

+Same district, opposite corners: packed district, so lots of zig-zagging through streets to get to her+

+I don't think I've ever walked more than a mile in my life+

Six miles. It didn't sound like very much at all.

+Can I keep this connection open with you, Concord? Blythe hasn't made a connection+

+Yes. It's not her fault. Her connections are few, and they're committed. Blythe's lovely. I think you'll really like her+

+I like her already. We managed to exchange a lot of personal information last week, but I'd like to talk to her more+

+You really think you're related?+

+I'm almost convinced of it+

+Thanks, Dharma. Forty minute lunch break, so I've got to go. Talk soon+

+Talk soon, Concord+

The screen blinked out, and Con switched to his company screen. Blythe turned at almost exactly the same moment.

"How's your mum?" he asked.

"The same," said Blythe. "How was your map?"

"Enlightening."

"Old maps are enlightening? Weird!"

"You're a bit weird, though, too, aren't you?"

"How do you mean?"

173

"You take a lot of shit from your mum, and it doesn't seem to bother you very much… You just take it."

"I've got broad shoulders," said Blythe, "and Mum has her reasons for being the way she is."

"You don't want to talk about it," said Con. "I get that."

"It's just that Joy should be back any minute, and I don't want to get into it, now. We can talk about it sometime, though, if you'd like. You shared details of your childhood with me, after all."

"Another time, then."

"She wants me to visit," said Blythe.

"And that's a problem?"

"I haven't been for a couple of years. It's a massive hassle."

"Different district? You're lucky. I've never been out of the district."

"You haven't missed much," said Blythe.

"Who hasn't missed what?" asked Joy, walking into the cubicle. "I'm sure you two are plotting something. I hope it's not to do with me."

"I can assure you it isn't," said Con.

"I don't trust you," said Joy.

"It's fine," said Blythe. "It's my fault, anyway."

"I could've guessed that," said Joy.

"Now listen, here," said Con. "I've had about enough of you. You've been nothing but mean to Blythe since she got here… and it's been three years. Why can't you just be nice for once in your life?"

"Con!" said Blythe

"What?" Asked Con.

"Too harsh. You don't know Joy's life. Cut her some slack, for goodness sake."

"Wow!" said Con. "You really are nice, aren't you?"

"I've got no reason not to be."

Joy sat at her station, staring at Blythe, blinking hard against the tears that were forming in the corners of her eyes.

Blythe looked from Con to Joy.

"Sorry, Joy," said Con.

"I'll forgive you this once," said Joy. "I just wish things could go back to the way they were. I don't know what happened while I was away, but things have changed, and I don't like it."

"Sorry," said Con, again, "but I guess you're just going to have to get used to it."

Forty-one

"Right," said Pa. "We need to get some things sorted out, as a matter of urgency."

"I'm not coming home," said Charity.

"I've been talking to your mother, and we're not going to make you come home… At least, not for the moment. You might be safer where you are, and the authorities have plenty to say about it. First of all, has Able been certified with immunity?"

"Yes, Pa," said Charity. "His dad was sick for a long time, and had all sorts of treatments. Able had it for a while but he had notification of his immunity before his dad died."

"Good. That's one less thing to worry about."

"You didn't take anything with you. Your mother says you didn't even pack an overnight bag."

"I left in Mum's dress and a pair of trainers," said Charity. "I wanted to be able to move fast. It seemed stupid to carry stuff."

"You were going to make a run for it, if a guard saw you."

"Only if I had to. Seems a bit stupid now."

"I'm glad you realise that. Now, you've obviously got your phone."

"I needed to be able to talk to you. I've got my id, too."

"Good," said Pa. "It means your rations can be delivered to you there. Do you know how that works?"

"Able's been filling in the requisition forms for his dad for a long time, so it should be straightforward. There are some personal things I'll need to add, but it's all set up."

"I've filled out your forms to let the authorities know that you're no longer living here. They phoned me up to find out whether there was an emergency, or a death, and why I hadn't filled in the relevant documentation."

"Oh," said Charity. "Sorry, Pa… I hope you didn't get into trouble."

"More to the point, I managed to keep you out of any trouble. I explained everything that's been going on, and I explained about you and Able, and his dad. I laid it on thick, told a real sob story."

"I can imagine," said Charity.

"Frankly, it wasn't difficult to shed a tear over the phone."

"I am sorry, Pa. I really am sorry, but it's for the best. You know it is."

"Anyway, the long and the short of it is that they're not going to impose any sanctions on you, on the understanding that you remain where you are. You're not allowed to move, Charity."

"That's okay. I don't want to move."

"I hope this relationship is everything you think it is. I want you to be happy, but I'm worried that you don't know this boy."

"Able," said Charity. "Call him Able… or Abe."

"I'm worried that you don't know Able, and that you'll end up miserable with each other. I can't think of anything worse than two people stuck in a house together, hating each other."

"That's not going to happen, I promise. Besides, you let Sage and Verity move down together."

"That's different."

"I don't see how."

"They'd known each other for longer, and they were older."

"I'm older than you think, Pa… Maybe not in years, but the Deluge has made me grow up fast."

"Too fast," said Pa.

"Besides, me and Abe probably did more talking about more things, while I was stuck at home, than Verity and Sage did in the whole two years they were dating, and they turned out all right."

"I suppose. I still worry that you're very young. And I hope you're being sensible."

"I've got my own little room," said Charity, "with its own single bed. We don't have to spend all our time together if we don't want to. This house is as big as ours, and there were five of us packed in there… We survived."

"I like to think we did very nicely."

"Me, too," said Charity. "Talking of 'five', how are Verity and the baby? How's the nursery coming along?"

Nik Abnett

"I decided not to do anything until I spoke to you and checked in with the authorities. I wanted to make sure you were settled first."

"Then you should get off the phone, and get on with building the baby a lovely nursery. You need a project."

"You're my project, today."

"It sounds as if I've been your project since I left. Thanks for sorting things out for me. That word 'sanctions' doesn't sound too pleasant."

"You don't want to know, but suffice to say that you wouldn't have been coming back here, and you wouldn't have been staying where you are, either, if the most severe sanctions had been imposed."

"You saved my life, Pa," said Charity.

"And now you owe me."

"Anything."

"You owe it to me to stay safe, and be happy, and not to get up to any shenanigans."

"I'm not the shenanigans type," said Charity, laughing.

"I've made some arrangements. I don't know what you're doing for clothes and things, but I put in a requisition with the nice official I talked to on the phone. The forms are all filled out."

"What's happening?"

"We're allowed to pack two cartons of your stuff, and they'll be fumigated and dropped off with your next rations."

"Oh, Pa. That's lovely of you, thank you."

"Don't thank me. Your mother's doing the hard work, going through your room, packing your clothes, and some other bits and pieces."

"Give her a kiss from me. And take one for yourself."

"This will all be over soon," said Pax. "We'll all get our immunisation shots and you'll be able to kiss me in person."

"I hope so," said Charity. "There isn't anything I really need, but it'd be nice to have some of my own stuff." She was thinking mostly about underwear. She didn't need socks in the warm summer weather, and she could borrow some from Able. Bras and knickers would be very useful, though. She didn't mind going without in the summer, but she'd need things when the weather turned cold again.

178

Sharing Abe's jeans and t-shirts was all well and good, but everything was a bit shapeless on her. Besides, she wanted the opportunity to look nice. Wearing her mother's dress, doing her hair and putting on some makeup had really cheered her up, the day of Verity's wedding. She didn't have any make-up with her, or a decent hairbrush. Mum would know what to pack.

"Let's talk again, tomorrow, then," said Pax. "You make sure you look after yourself."

"I promise."

"And you could say hello to Able from me. I'll want to get to know him."

"You'll like him... You really will."

"If he's good enough for you, he's good enough for us."

"Love you, Pa. Talk tomorrow."

"Bye, Darling. Love you too."

Able wandered into the kitchen as Charity finished her call.

"Pa says hi," she said.

"He's okay with it, then? Because I don't think I could bear to give you up now."

"The authorities won't allow it anyway," said Charity. "I'll make a cup of tea, and tell you all about it."

Forty-two

Dharma had enjoyed her personal project, but she decided that there was much more that she could do. She had begun to be fascinated by her entire family, and any information she could add would only back up what she already knew.

She was almost sure that this really was her family, but almost wasn't sure enough.

Every lunch time for the next few weeks, Dharma accessed pre-Deluge records to find more of her family, more generations going further back in time. She began by following Faith Bigelow's line, and when she had gone as far as she could, she had a beautiful family tree, filled with dozens of surnames and hundreds of people.

Some of the families going back to the early twentieth century and even earlier had several children. They didn't all survive into adulthood, but some did, and there were more branches to follow.

Dharma also began to look at infant mortality, and average life expectancy, and all sorts of other statistics that she could scrutinise and analyse.

The World before the Deluge had been a strange and, it seemed to Dharma, often horrible place. Children died, and the life expectancy of adults was low. People had strange occupations that she had never heard of and couldn't imagine.

Nevertheless, people obviously found love, and married, and did the sex thing. Constance Tuke, Dharma's grandmother, had been right about a lot of the things she had talked about in her stories. Dharma understood that her grandmother had been born before the Deluge, and that the World had been very different then. She wondered how many stories Verity had told to her daughter about her own family's life, and how much of them Constance had believed.

Verity's side of the family had always lived in the Catford area. She even found a relation who had served in the World War, back in the 1940s, a member of the 101st Regiment of the Royal Engineers.

There was no royal family in the New Wave. Most of the senior royals had died during the Deluge, and the junior members opted out of the old system. Dharma couldn't find out why that had happened, but Monarchy seemed a strange system. Still, she'd had a relation who'd 'fought for King and Country', and, somehow, that made her feel good. There was courage in her ancestry.

When Dharma couldn't find out any more information about Faith Bigelow's family, she decided to follow Pax Mott's lineage. She still didn't trust paternity, but she got caught up in the hunt. She'd got the hang of following the data trails, and was able to verify members of his family through birth, marriage and death certificates, census records and even professional organisations. She even found some of the places that they had lived, and tracked them on old maps. She discovered where Leeds was. It was more than two hundred miles north of Bromley, and she wondered why, or how, anyone could travel that far. She knew that some goods were transported over long distances, but people, individuals didn't travel.

The further Dharma went back through the generations, the more people seemed to stay in one place for long periods of time.

She began to look into the history of transport. She knew about goods vehicles, and she'd seen cars in old movies, but now she found out about the national railway system and the underground trains in London. One of Pax's relatives had been a 'railwayman', one of the many professions that she neither knew existed nor understood what the job entailed. She had not known about aeroplanes, nor that people had travelled on them en-masse. Suddenly, two hundred miles was nothing. People had travelled across the World, on flights that could take several hours. They'd done it for almost a hundred years, between the War and the Deluge. But when she found out that a man had once stood on the moon, she simply didn't believe it. The idea stretched her capacity to suspend her disbelief, beyond breaking point.

Dharma decided that the New Wave must be much more like the old way of doing things, that the twenty-second century more closely resembled the eighteenth than any period in between. Except for one fundamental thing: in the eighteenth century people had not lived alone. She could not find a time in history, going through thousands of old census records, when people had. People, it seemed, always lived in family units, usually of two generations, and often of three. There were outliers, of course, but there were always outliers.

The Deluge had turned the clock back in some ways, and it had changed human existence forever in others.

Human life endured, though. It seemed to Dharma, with her huge cache of old records and documents, that life had always endured, and that people were capable of things that she had never imagined. People were capable of almost anything.

Forty-three

"That's the rations arriving," Able called out, peering out of the front window, as the van pulled up outside.

The driver was in a paper suit, with a cap, mask, gloves, and protective eye-wear. He began to unload covered plastic crates from the van onto the drive. He sprayed each one with sanitiser from a bottle at his belt, once he'd put it down. And, finally, he picked up the empties and took them back to the van.

"There are lots of boxes," he called again. "Come and see."

Charity came out of the kitchen, wiping her hands on a cloth. She stood next to Able, at the window and looked at the boxes.

"Pa did it!" she said. "He promised he'd organised things, but I didn't want to believe it until I saw for myself."

"It's your stuff!" said Abe, realising what was going on. "Is your father a miracle worker by any chance?"

"He knows how to talk nicely to people. I can't remember a time when he couldn't get things done."

"Well, good for him."

"Good for me," said Charity, leaving the living room.

The driver had pulled away from in front of the house, and Charity walked out without a second thought. She had already picked up the first of her boxes when Able came to the door in a paper suit, mask and gloves.

"We're immune," said Charity. "We don't need to do any of that any more. In fact, if you check the rations, I'm not expecting to find any more protective gear."

"Oh." Abe pulled his face mask down. "Now I feel ridiculous."

Charity laughed.

"Come and give me a hand," she said.

All of Charity's favourite clothes were neatly folded in one of the boxes, including freshly laundered underwear, a robe, and even a sweater and a jacket for when the weather turned. It was the height of summer, so Charity assumed that Pa had insisted on the jacket, just in case. Surely the Deluge would be over before another winter had passed. Faith had also packed Charity's favourite bed linen. Her mum had gone above and beyond to make sure that Charity was happy and had familiar things around her. She opened the second box and found some more of her personal things: a make-up bag and hairbrush, a soft toy she'd had since she was a child, a couple of her favourite books, and some other bits and pieces. There was a ring box tucked in a corner that Charity didn't recognise. She opened it.

She thought for a moment that she was going to cry. Faith had given Verity her eternity ring when she had married Sage. This box contained her engagement ring. There was a note with it, folded small and tucked into the box-lid.

"Don't get any funny ideas," it said. "I just wanted you to have something personal of mine while you're away. I hope you'll wear it. Love, Mum X."

Charity slipped the ring onto the fourth finger on her right hand. It wasn't for her and Able, it was for her and Mum.

There was also a large, fat manila envelope in the box, with something written on the outside.

"Should we unpack, inside?" asked Able, as he watched Charity rummaging around in the boxes while they still stood on the drive. He'd already taken the rations into the kitchen for unpacking.

"Sorry. Yes, that's a good idea." She popped the lids back on the boxes and picked up the one with the clothes in it. Able took the other one and they headed inside.

Charity went upstairs with her box, unpacked her clothes and put them away in the spare room where the drawers and wardrobe were empty. She also changed the sheets on the bed to her own bed linen. When she was finished, it felt so like the old box room that she'd spent so much time in for the past several months, she almost wanted to cry again.

While Charity was upstairs, Able had unpacked the rations boxes and put everything away.

"Anything good?" asked Charity, as she wandered into the kitchen.

"No real milk, this time, but there's a can of the powdered stuff."

"Well that's not good," said Charity.

"It is when it's mixed with this." Able held up a small drum of cocoa powder. "We can have hot chocolate, or cold milkshakes."

"Milkshakes, please."

"You realise we'll have to make the hot chocolate and then refrigerate it until it becomes cold milkshake, right?"

"I know how this stuff works," she said, smiling. "I can wait."

"Milkshakes it is," said Able, finding a measuring jug and a saucepan, and setting to work.

"Are you all set up in your room?" he asked, as Charity sat and watched him work.

"It's lovely. Mum even sent my favourite duvet cover."

"Good. What's in the other box?"

"Oh! I'd forgotten about the other box. Where did you put it?"

"By the front door."

Charity fetched it, putting it on the kitchen table to unpack. She made a little ritual of it. Starting with her mother's ring, she showed each item to Abe, telling him where it had come from and why it was important to her.

"What's in the envelope?" he asked. He'd finished making the cocoa and was standing at the table with Charity.

"I don't know." She turned it over to read what was written on the outside, and laughed.

"What's funny?" asked Able.

"It's from Sage," she said. "From him and Mum."

She opened the envelope and tipped the contents out onto the table. A dozen or more little brown envelopes landed in a haphazard pile. Able picked one up at random. The block capital handwriting on the outside said, 'spinach'. He picked up another one. It said 'nasturtiums'.

"I hope you know how to garden," he said, "because I haven't got a clue. I might be able to find some old tools in the shed, but it's all lawn back there."

Charity pushed her hand into the envelope, almost up to the elbow, and pulled out a folded piece of paper.

"Don't worry," she said, unfolding the paper and waving it under his nose. "We've got instructions."

185

Forty-four

"Do you have any plans for the weekend?" asked Con.

"What do you mean, plans?" asked Blythe.

"I've got to see my mother," said Joy.

"You see," said Con. "That's a plan."

"My mother's been trying to persuade me to visit her, but it's such a pain, and I'd never get everything sorted by the weekend," said Blythe. "It's Wednesday already. Maybe I'll put through the forms and go next month."

"Other plans, then?" asked Concord.

"For instance?"

"Sometimes I read a book."

"A nineteenth century novel," said Blythe.

"Or twentieth century Science Fiction. There's some good stuff."

"It's not real, though is it?" asked Joy. "None of it's real."

"That's sort of the point."

"I like that thing they stream, about the people in the cubicle," said Joy.

"I think it's called 'The Cubicle'," said Blythe, smiling at Con while Joy's back was turned.

"That's the one," said Joy, missing the irony.

"So, you sit with us in a cubicle all week, and then you go home to watch people sitting in a cubicle on streaming."

"But there are only three of us," said Joy. "There are four of them in 'The Cubicle'."

"Yes, there are," said Con. "I don't watch a lot of streaming, but sometimes I like to take a walk."

"Really?" asked Joy, turning her chair to look at him. "Why would you do that?"

"I like it."

"Well," said Joy, turning her chair back to her station. "I think that's weird."

"Then you and Blythe have something in common," said Con. "Because she thinks I'm weird, too."

"I used to think you were nice."

Blythe raised an eyebrow at Con, but said nothing.

"I walk every day," he said. "Well, most days anyway, for forty minutes."

"During your lunch break," Blythe remembered.

"You could walk a long way in forty minutes," said Joy. "You could cross the district border if you walk for forty minutes. That's terrifying."

"I walk around and around," said Con. "I never walk in a straight line during lunch."

"I eat during lunch," said Joy. "The people at the lunch bar are nice… Nicer than you two."

"I'm sure they are," said Blythe.

"Anyway," said Con. "I thought I might take a walk this weekend, or maybe next weekend. I wondered if I could persuade you to go with me?"

"Not a chance," said Joy.

Con raised an eyebrow at Blythe; she knew he wasn't asking Joy.

"I might," said Blythe, even though it made her feel nervous.

Blythe and Con had found a way to talk to each other, while apparently having a general conversation in the cubicle with Joy. Neither of them wanted to go back to the way it had been before Joy's holiday. Ideally, Joy would be a better fit, but, she wasn't. So, Blythe and Con talked to each other, and if Joy chimed in, that was fine. It also seemed to keep Joy a bit happier, and there wasn't as much conversational room for her complaints when Blythe or Con set the agenda for their chats.

"Well, you two can plan your weekend walk while I go to my lunch bar," said Joy, logging out of Anley Corp's intranet. The screen faded to black, and Joy left the cubicle.

"How far do you think you could walk?" asked Con.

"I don't know, I've never thought about it."

"What floor of your building do you live on?"

"The sixth."

187

"Wow!" said Con. "You got unlucky."

"Actually, there's a trick to it. When I was looking for housing I did quite a bit of research. There are always things we can do to work the system."

"I don't get it. You *chose* to live on the sixth floor?"

"I live in an old building, converted after the Deluge."

"Well, obviously," said Con. "None of the modern buildings are higher than three storeys."

"But, they're built for purpose."

"Yes?"

"What do you know about old buildings?"

"Not much. I haven't been in many."

"Which market do you use?"

"Brewers."

"Oh…" said Blythe. "Same… Okay, so you know the layout of an old building. Hasn't it ever crossed your mind that the spaces are big, and the ceilings are high?"

"Well, some are."

"Next time you go, have a look at what's original and where partitions have been added to divide up the space."

"I will," said Con, "but what's that got to do with you choosing to live on the sixth floor?"

"When people fill in housing forms, what do they prioritise?"

"The lower three floors, obviously. It's the first box everyone ticks."

"What floor is your apartment on?" asked Blythe.

"The first. I didn't want to be on the ground floor."

"And how big is it?"

"I guess it's the same as most singles. Why?"

"You've got a murphy bed, or a sleeping platform?"

"A platform," said Con, "but don't we all?"

"We don't," said Blythe. "Here's the thing. Nobody wants to climb up and down stairs more than they absolutely have to, and there's no other way to reach higher floors in buildings."

"Right," said Con.

"Mothers don't want to have to carry babies up several flights of stairs, either."

"Right."

"So everyone wants to live on the bottom three floors of a building. There's a high demand. Are you with me, Concord?"

"So far."

"The purpose-built apartment blocks give each occupant the minimum space they can live in, hence murphy beds, kitchenettes, wet rooms. Most apartments are studios."

"Right, again."

"Old buildings converted into apartments use the same principle. They partition up the space on the lowest three floors into single units or small apartments for mothers with a child."

"Yes," said Con.

"They don't do that further up the old buildings."

"How do you mean?"

"If nobody wants to live on the sixth floor, what's the point of spending time and money partitioning that floor into small studios?"

"There is no point, I suppose."

"Which is why they don't do it," said Blythe. "The sixth floor of my building has not been partitioned up, so I have a sitting room, a bedroom, a kitchen and a bathroom."

"That can't be true," said Con.

"My apartment is huge," said Blythe, smiling.

"Why didn't I know about this?"

"You could always put in a request for relocation. Plenty of people would be happy to take your little studio rather than live above the third floor."

"I might just do that. I feel foolish not knowing about it."

"Well, let's keep it a secret between the two of us… We don't want everyone jumping on this particular bandwagon."

"Six flights of stairs, though," said Con. "Up, and down."

"Five, actually," said Blythe. "It took me a while to get used to it but, honestly, it makes me feel good. I look forward to trotting down my stairs every morning."

"I'm pretty sure you could walk a decent distance, then, if you had to," said Con. "If you wanted to."

"I suppose I could. Outside, though, for a long time… Is that a good idea?"

"I don't know, but maybe we should find out."

"You have been plotting," said Blythe. "Joy was right all along."

"By the law of averages, she had to be right about something eventually."

"You want us to go for a walk together, this weekend?"

"Hopefully this weekend, if I can work out a good route," said Con. "It might be next weekend."

"Well, I'm always free," said Blythe. "Don't expect me to like it, though, it's making me feel anxious just thinking about it."

"I'll plan properly. I'll do my research, and I promise I'll keep you safe," said Con. "It's just an experiment."

"An experiment you don't want to do on your own?"

"It's an experiment that involves you," said Con. "As a matter of fact. It's an experiment that I can't do without you."

"So, you're really asking me to do you a favour?" asked Blythe.

"I'm asking you to do us both a favour."

"I'd have done it anyway. You're the nearest thing I've got to a friend, and when a friend asks for something it's churlish to refuse."

"Churlish?" asked Con.

"I've struggled with it a bit, but I started reading *Great Expectations*, because you said Dickens was good. I spend a lot of time looking words up."

"There's no need. Context is everything, and Dickens is good at context. Just read it, and you'll soon get the hang of it."

"It's like a foreign language," said Blythe.

"It really isn't," said Con, smiling.

Forty-five

Dharma went for her jog the following Saturday, mid-morning, around the same time she'd gone when she'd met Patience in the gardens.

The morning was fresh and bright, and the jog was easy. Dharma enjoyed it. She held her id up to the scanner, and was let in. She walked around the garden, to the back of the building, and looked up at the rooms where her mother used to live. The window box was in full bloom. She could see splashes of orange, and lots of greenery, some of it hanging down a metre or so.

She sat in the grass for a few minutes, thinking about her mother, and about all the women in her mother's family that she had come to know something about over the past few months.

She got up, and walked over to the deep flower bed, where the geraniums were growing.

"Help yourself," someone said from behind her. Dharma turned to see Patience in her beekeeping outfit, her headgear under one arm. "I grow lots of them, and they bloom all summer long. They make good companion plants."

"I don't understand anything about plants," said Dharma. "What's a companion plant?"

"Some plants repel the pests that would otherwise eat other plants," said Patience. "If I grow geraniums close to cabbages and broccoli, they keep the cabbage worms from eating my crop."

"Clever," said Dharma. "I didn't know."

"I bet you know lots of other things," said Patience, smiling.

"I was wondering about the orange flowers."

"You might have to be more specific."

"The window box of my mother's old apartment. There are orange flowers in it. I don't recognise them," said Dharma.

"Marigolds. Look over there." She pointed to a large patch of the orange flowers.

"Yes," said Dharma.

191

"They're around the potato patch."

"They keep something off your potatoes?" asked Dharma.

"Tomatoes, too."

"What about the bees? You collect the honey?"

"I keep them to pollinate the plants," said Patience. "You must have taken some basic science school?"

"I was always more of a physicist than a chemist or horticulturalist. I'm a data analyst."

"So am I, in a way. I've been working this garden for ten years, making notes of what grows best where, and which companion plants are the most effective. How to get the best range of produce growing year round to feed my people."

"The residents?" asked Dharma.

"Who else? Your mother died… It was a while ago."

"Yes, nearly two years. Is there a problem?"

"I don't know. I suppose it's fine. You aren't doing any harm. You're welcome whenever you like. I don't get many visitors in the garden."

"The residents don't come down here? I thought my mother did."

"She did, and Libby still comes down most days. She stays in at the weekends to talk to her daughter, so you're the only person I've seen on a Saturday for a long time."

"I didn't mean to disturb you," said Dharma.

"You haven't," said Patience, smiling. "It's always nice to see someone… Two years since your mother died, you said."

"Almost. The anniversary's just a few weeks away."

"Well," said Patience, "all the time your id gets you into the garden, you're very welcome here."

"Thanks."

"And think about growing something," said Patience. "I can give you all the seeds you'll need for a window box."

"I will," said Dharma. She picked some geraniums, and walked away towards the gate. When she reached it, she turned and looked back at the main entrance to the building. She stood for a minute, thinking, and then she walked up to the door and showed her id to the scanner. The door opened. Dharma stood in front of it for a few moments, not knowing quite what to do, since she had no one to visit. Then she turned and the door closed.

She jogged home, quite comfortably, and only passed through the wipe at the entrance to her building, once. When she got home, she went into her living room, and crossed the room to the window. Her shower could wait for a minute. Dharma reached for the handle, and the window swung open, easily, on its hinge. She pulled the window back towards her, and the inertia kept it there, open just a little.

Dharma left the window while she went to take her shower. When she'd dressed and come back into the room with her cup of geraniums, the window was just as she'd left it. Nothing in the room seemed to have changed at all.

Perhaps she would have a window box, one of these days.

Forty-six

"She's gone," said Con. "She took a transfer."

"What do you mean, she took a transfer? And who are we talking about?" asked Blythe.

"Anley Corp has cubicles in another building near here, and Joy asked to be transferred. Apparently, she's been looking for a station in a cubicle of four for a while now."

"Well, good for her."

"Someone's coming to remove her station overnight, so we'll have a bit more space."

"That makes no sense. This is a three person cubicle."

"We get an extra connection, too," said Con. "We have to share it, though. I couldn't get it allocated to you, but I got a two-thirds split, so you get it for two weeks out of three. It means you can speak to Dharma, without giving up your old friend."

"Back up," said Blythe. "You realise that I don't have a clue what's going on, here?"

"I'm ninetieth percentile," said Con.

"And you do like to brag about that, don't you?"

"You've earned enough incentive and bonus points to bump you up to eightieth percentile."

"So?"

"So, I got you a promotion," said Con. "It didn't take much, I just filled out the form."

"Aren't I supposed to do that?"

"We key-in, here, and I know your id."

"You pretended to be me!" said Blythe.

"It sounds appalling now that you say it. I was trying to do a nice thing, and I was trying to keep a third person out of the cubicle."

"Weren't you the one who said 'a change is as good as a rest'?"

"I believe I might have said that, at some point. Here's the upside: you get to do more interesting work, you get an extra connection two weeks out of three, and we get a little more space in this cubicle… and a little more privacy."

"And the downside?" asked Blythe.

"As far as I'm concerned, there is no downside. But if there's a downside for you, let me know, and I'll do my best to fix it. Anley Corp likes me, especially now that I've promised to un-demote myself, and do some higher level stuff for them."

"I thought you had to be in a single to do that," said Blythe.

"Not if you sign some forms saying you won't divulge any proprietary data. You're eightieth percentile now, and I vouched for you."

"And you think I want that kind of responsibility?" asked Blythe.

"I know you're better than the job you're doing, and I know you're on auto. You'll get much more fun out of the work this way. It gets pretty interesting."

"Okay, assuming I go along with that…There has to be a downside."

"Oh," said Con. "There is one other thing."

"Go on."

"You can adjust your tariff. You've gone up a pay scale."

Blythe was smiling, but cautious.

"So what is it you want from me?" she asked.

"Nothing," said Con. "But if you did want to return the favour, you have been putting off taking that walk with me for weeks now."

"Ah," said Blythe, "there's the downside. I have to take a long walk with you one weekend."

"You don't have to, but you've agreed to it, in principle, several times, and you always back out at the last minute."

"It doesn't scare you?" asked Blythe.

"It really doesn't. It's completely safe. I've planned a route and I know where we're going. I've even booked two seats at a lunch bar, so that we can take a break when we get to the district line."

"And there it is!" said Blythe.

"You're afraid to cross the district line," said Con.

"I'm afraid to cross the district line without proper authorisation. Aren't you?"

"No, and I'll tell you why. We aren't putting in requisition forms for route assignment or for transport. Transport has to pass through quarantine wipes, and you need proper authorisation for that."

"And?" asked Blythe.

"And, if we're walking, we don't have to pass through the quarantine wipes."

"And if we get caught?"

"Then, we're just out for a walk, and we didn't realise we'd crossed the line."

"Do you seriously think anyone's going to believe that?" asked Blythe.

"I seriously believe that no one's going to stop us to ask."

"This really doesn't scare you?"

"It really doesn't scare me," said Con. "I'm n–"

"Ninetieth percentile. Yes, I know. But does that make you clever enough to break the law and get away with it?"

"We aren't breaking any laws by walking around. We'd only be breaking a law if we deviated from assigned routes, or hi-jacked transport. We haven't been assigned a route, and I had no plans to steal transport. I wouldn't know how to drive, anyway."

"You're confident we wouldn't be breaking any laws?"

"Utterly confident," he said. "Look, we'll go through it all, together. I'll show you some of the old maps, and you can see how route-planning works. It's easy. Nothing can go wrong. You just have to know where you are and where you're going."

"And you know where we're going, hypothetically?"

"I do. I'm sorry that I can't tell you where that is, but I know exactly where we're going and why."

"Okay. I'll think about it some more, and I'll let you show me how those old maps work... After that, I'll think about it, again.

"That's all I ask," said Con.

"And I've got another connection for two weeks out of three?"

"You can open your connection with Dharma today, and talk to her as much as you like."

"Good," said Blythe.

When it was time for lunch, Con got up from his station, and pulled a sweater over his head. Blythe often wondered why he wore a sweater, even on hot days.

"I feel like a walk, today," he said. "You can have all the privacy you need to talk to Dharma. I'll bring back coffee."

"Thanks," said Blythe. It had been a long morning, filling out non-disclosure forms, working through instruction manuals, and doing tests, for her to learn her new job. It was exciting though, and she didn't, for one moment, miss the Anley Corp invoice template.

Blythe opened her connection to Dharma, and they talked for half an hour. Blythe had managed to read through a lot of the data that Dharma had sent her, but she was more interested in the personal stories, in who Dharma was, and what she was like. She asked about how Dharma had found her, too.

+I have good access to records, as part of my job+

+Personal records?+

+I've done some data analysis for good genetic matches, so some medical records, yes+

+That's how you found me?+

+Your id was on your mother's medical record+

+You know things about me and Mum+

+Only data…+

+You paused, Dharma, what aren't you telling me?+

+Nothing… You're very lucky to be here, Blythe, and I feel very lucky to have you here+

+Yes+

+Did Liberty, your mum, tell you anything about your birth?+

+My mother can be difficult… demanding. I love her, but she's too invested in me. I always disappoint+

+Don't be too hard on her+

+Why not? I've had to live with her my entire life. She makes me anxious about everything. There's something I'd really like to do, but I'm afraid.+

+I've started to walk around the gardens of my mother's old senior housing. I pick flowers and talk to the gardener… I would

197

never have done that while my mother was alive. I miss her, though.+

+What are you saying?+

+I don't know. Look at the data I sent you. I've got more, if you're interested. It's made me think about time and change. The New Wave is a safe place compared to everything that came before. We have good jobs and comfortable homes, and, now, you and I have this+

+Millions died!+

+And a couple of generations later, we can learn to live again... I think we're living in a better World. Look at the data, Blythe, and we'll talk some more about it.+

+It's good to meet you Dharma. I'll go through the data. Con can help me make better sense of it+

+He's clever, and insightful, and nice. You can rely on him+

+What do you mean? How do you know Con?+

+We have a permanent connection, since you gave me his id to send the converted source material. We speak often. He took some intuitive leaps that helped me find more information.+

+You speak to each other? I didn't know+

+Sorry, Blythe, perhaps I shouldn't have said anything+

+Perhaps Con should have said something to me+

+Don't be angry with him. He's a good guy, and my favourite connection+

+You're friends, Dharma?+

+Good friends. You should be friends with him, too, Blythe+

+I think I am, but he pushes me to do things that make me uncomfortable+

+Like your mother?+

+No, the opposite. He wants me to do the sort of things that my mother would always warn me against+

+Perhaps Con can give you a little of the confidence you say your mother robbed you of... We don't really know each other, but I think your mother had a difficult life. I think she wanted yours to be easy+

+So she stopped me from doing anything+

+Perhaps she was just keeping you safe. Perhaps she couldn't bear to lose you+

+Perhaps... You think I should trust Con?+

+I think I'd trust him... In fact, I know I would+

+Thanks, Dharma+

+Let's speak again, soon, Blythe. This connection's permanently open to you+

+Thanks, but my connection is shared with Con, so I can only use it two weeks in three. You'll soon be tired of me, anyway.+

+We're relations, and you're the only one I have. Don't worry, I won't tire of you. Bye Blythe.+

+Bye Dharma+

"I've got a bone to pick with you, Concord Penn," said Blythe, almost before the cubicle door had closed behind him.

Con put her coffee on her station.

"Okay," he said. "What have I done?"

"You have an open connection to Dharma."

"Yes. We were working together on your family data... *Your* family, Blythe."

"She likes you."

"And I like her. We think a lot alike. We solved some puzzles together."

"And you talked about me?"

"Well, no actually. We didn't really talk about you."

"So what did you talk about?"

"Data," said Con. "Mostly we just talked about data."

The cubicle fell silent for a moment.

"Why are you angry?"

"Because I knew this would happen," said Blythe. "When I gave her your code, I knew that you'd take advantage."

"She doesn't want a relationship with me," said Con. "Yes, we talk about data, and we're interested in the same sort of stuff, but I'm not her cousin... You are. Dharma came looking for you, and I helped her to find you. That's all there is to it."

"I don't know why it's upset me. It's stupid. You've got no mother and no connections. There's no reason you shouldn't talk to Dharma. I'm sorry. I wish you'd told me, though."

"It seemed cruel. You couldn't open a connection to Dharma but I could. I didn't want to gloat about it, so I just didn't tell you."

"Have you kept any other secrets from me, Con?"

"I don't think so. I'm still not going to tell you where we're going on our walk, but apart from that I'm not keeping any secrets. And, honestly, I haven't told you any lies."

"You swear?"

"Swear. I like you, Blythe, and I have two more people in my life than I've ever had before."

"Good. Now, can you explain this chapter of the training manual to me, because some of this Anley Corp jargon is impenetrable, and I want to make sure I understand."

"Absolutely," said Con.

And they went back to work.

Forty-seven

"Hi Pa," said Charity, checking her watch. "Is everything okay? It's very early."

"Verity had the baby! Half an hour ago. Your mother told me not to phone yet; she said you'd be asleep, but I couldn't wait any longer."

"Oh, Pa, that's lovely," said Charity, nudging Able, and when he turned bleary eyed towards her, putting a finger to her lips, gesturing him to be quiet. "Is Verity okay? Is the baby? What about Mum?"

"It went by the book, according to your mother. Sage was there, holding Verity's hand, and it all went very quickly. He came to find your mother a little before midnight, and she was here a little after five o'clock."

"It's a girl?" She gave Able a thumbs-up.

"A little girl, about seven pounds. They've decided to call her Constance. Sage, Verity and the baby are all tucked up in their room, your mother's lying down, and I've done some cleaning up. I had to ring you."

"I'm glad you did, Pa. Give everyone my love."

"And you're all right?" asked Pax. "I know we speak every day, and it's been three months, but we worry about you."

"How long has it been?" asked Charity, smiling.

"Seventeen weeks and four days. Just tell me you're all right, Charity, and stop teasing."

"I couldn't be better. Check in with you later, when I'm actually awake."

"Bye darling, love you."

"Love you, too, Pa. And give my niece a kiss from her aunty."

"Will do," said Pax, before hanging up.

Charity put her phone back on the bedside table, and turned to put her arms around Able.

"Morning mouth," warned Able.

"Don't care," said Charity, kissing him.

"It's October, already," said Able, "almost November. "It's going to start getting cold."

"Have they decided whether we're turning the clocks back, tonight? I'm still not clear on that."

"Does it matter?"

"Well, not to us," said Charity, "but there are key workers out there who could do with the extra hour of sleep."

"What about those who'll have an extra hour added to their shifts?"

"Pessimist."

"Realist."

"Let's be optimists, today," she said, smiling. "There's baby Constance to think about now."

"Do you suppose that will ever be us?"

"The rate we're going through condoms, who knows," said Charity, smiling again. "If we run out before the next rations, are you going to be able to contain yourself?"

"No, I mean it. One day, I want us to get married and have children."

"We might want to finish our educations first."

"I've already started," said Able. "I've been doing some university courses on the education website."

"All that reading? I thought you were doing that to avoid having to talk to me all day long."

"To avoid the gardening." He smiled. "But, seriously, I've been doing it so that I can make a life for us, once this is all over."

"They think it'll be soon, now," said Charity. "The number of new cases is negligible, and the vaccine's gone into trials."

"That visit from hazmat to take some samples from us was all worth it then. I'm glad we could help."

"They haven't disclosed the final death toll, yet, though… It's going to be a lot, isn't it?"

"Yes, it's going to be a lot. We've all lost someone."

"Sorry. I didn't mean to open wounds. You think about him, don't you? Although, you don't talk about him much."

"I imagine he's just in the next room, and can hear what we're saying. He would've really liked you, Charity... He would've flirted with you, too... He would've liked to see us like this."

"He wouldn't have liked the noises in the night."

"Trust me," said Able, "if my father was sleeping along the landing, I wouldn't let you make those noises."

"It's your fault," said Charity.

Able leaned across the kitchen table, and kissed her.

"Could that ever be us... Like Sage and Verity?" Able asked again.

"And Constance," said Charity.

"And Constance," said Able.

"I've grown up a lot since the Deluge. We both have. We're lucky, and we should make the best of it whatever the world looks like once this is all over. Besides, someone's got to repopulate."

"I was reading some statistics about that, too," said Able. "I think, at the end of this, there are going to be population controls."

"You reckon? Tell me some of the clever stuff you've been learning about."

"Are you mocking me?" asked Able, smiling.

"Not even a little bit," said Charity.

"I've been reading some modern philosophy stuff. Essays mostly, from people in the field who've been spending the past couple of years thinking about the implications of all this. People who are cleverer than I am."

"Weird," said Charity. "You're such a geek I didn't expect you to be interested in philosophy."

"It's remarkably pragmatic, and it's backed up by lots of statistical and ecological data collected since the Deluge started."

"Okay. Talk to me about that... You think they'll stop us having babies?"

"Consumption of the World's natural resources has dropped dramatically since the start of the outbreak.

"Because of the drop in population?"

"That's part of it, but there are other factors. People's lifestyles have changed beyond recognition over the past eighteen months."

"Two years," said Charity.

"Yes," said Able. "Two years, but the data isn't all current, yet. Anyway, lifestyle changes have caused dramatic improvements to the ozone layer, massively decreased use of fuels, and there's a much lower production of waste per capita of the population."

"Okay, but won't people simply go back to their old habits once the curfew is lifted, and we can all go about our business?"

"Time is the other factor," he said.

"Time?"

"Time's important for breaking and embedding habits."

"Okay, tell me about that," said Charity.

"Take alcohol," said Able. "Drinking alcohol is a tough habit to break if you're used to having a glass of wine every night."

"I suppose so. Pa found a bottle of sparkling wine so that we could toast Sage and Verity when they got married. It's the only alcohol any of us have had in almost two years."

"That's because there's no alcohol in the rations," said Able. "So, for some people, giving up their daily glass of wine was probably difficult and a bit frustrating to start with."

"I get that."

"Do you suppose your parents miss wine, now?"

"I don't remember them ever mentioning it."

"So they've broken the habit of drinking wine, and they've got into the habit of not drinking wine. It's a new pattern in their lives. The same goes for food. We all eat whatever comes in the rations. We don't think about it, we don't complain, and we're not fussy. We also consume everything. There were a huge number of complaints about food provision when the rations started. Everybody hated it at the beginning, but nobody thinks about it any more, and there's virtually no waste."

"Except for vegetable peelings and eggshells and stuff. Mum puts them on the compost heap, for the garden," said Charity.

"That's another thing," said Able. "Lots of people have got into the habit of gardening. They're not just producing food for their families, they're also enriching the environment. Added to which, their food isn't being transported, so less fuel is being used."

"Mum loves gardening, Sage, too, and I'd miss it if I stopped, even though most of what we've grown is salad greens and herbs."

"You're starting to make my point for me. These are all good habits that are becoming embedded in the population.

"Finally," he said, "there's the government."

"What about it?"

"When things started to look bad, at the beginning of all this, we had adversarial politics, when everyone was out for himself, everyone had an agenda and they were all capitalists."

"Sounds about right," said Charity.

"That's changed. Now, we have something more like proportional representation. We have an entire parliament, working together to get through a crisis."

"A bit like war-time," she said. "Did I mention I like history?"

"A bit like that. Politicians saw people dying, people close to them, and people started to ask questions about the vulnerable and the homeless. The government had to address those concerns in ways that they hadn't been addressed before.

"If the Deluge had been over in three months, say, then things probably would have gone back to the way they were, and quickly, too, but it's been two years."

"And?" asked Charity.

"We've broken old habits and adopted better ones. We've begun to repair the planet, and… And this is really critical. We've stopped questioning the motives of those who govern us. We trust them."

"Won't they take advantage of that trust, though?"

"Probably," said Able, "but what if they take advantage in such a way as to ensure an equitable society for the future? What if everyone is comfortable, can work, has enough to live on. What if everyone was housed, according to their need? What if there was no more child poverty?"

"Do you think they'd actually do it?" asked Charity. "That's not how governments have worked… ever, as far as I know."

"Who knows? Maybe they will take advantage. But we've all lost people, including everyone in the government. We've also lost the oldest and most conservative members of our communities in vast numbers."

"Old people dying is good?" asked Charity.

"Nobody dying is good, but younger voters have tended to be more liberal, more socially conscious, and more environmentally aware. Us, and all our school friends, will get to vote in the next election, and you know how much we've changed since this all started. Two years is a long time for teenagers."

"So, you're saying that the Deluge was a good thing?"

"I'm saying that there are cleverer people than me out there, speculating that the Deluge might have been instrumental in saving the planet, and if the planet is saved then the human race can go on for generations... Just in new, more responsible ways."

"And you think it's true?"

"I'm hoping it's true," said Able, "with one exception."

"And what's that?"

"The idea that population control could be introduced. The Chinese tried it once, back in the twentieth century. They had a one child policy. The results are still being talked about in some philosophical circles, but over all they were mixed, not least because there was an industrial revolution happening at the same time. So maybe it was all a wash, as far as the planet's concerned."

"That all sounds a bit speculative."

"It is, and I've only dipped a toe into the research, so I don't really have an opinion yet. There is a precedent, though, for population control."

"And you think we'll have it here?"

"I think it's a definite possibility, in the long term. One day I'd like to have a family with you, Charity. It was always just me and Dad, and it's hard to grow up like that, no matter how much you love each other. We should have two children, at least."

"Maybe, one day," said Charity. "Can we wait and see what happens, at least for a while?"

"Of course we can. It'll take a decade, or longer, to implement any of the most extreme changes, according to the stuff I'm reading... I think they're wrong. I think changes will be made quite quickly to stay in line with current laws."

"The interim laws?"

"I think there'll be a push for them to become permanent, almost as soon as the Deluge is over. After that, it's anybody's guess how quickly new laws will come into force that affect our everyday lives. Some choices might be taken away from us."

"Okay," said Charity. "I love you, but I'm not ready to have your child."

"And I'm good with that," said Able, "but we might have to talk about it some more, sooner than we think."

"We'll cross that bridge when we get to it then."

"Let's say we'll talk about it again when they start building the bridge."

"Agreed. Now, can we talk about something a bit less serious? "What do you want to try growing next?"

"According to Faith, we should be planting, broad beans and cauliflower, and some peas?"

"I hate broad beans."

"More for me," said Able. "Now get a sweater, and we'll go out in the garden for a couple of hours."

Forty-eight

Blythe and Concord sat together in a booth, in the lunch-bar that Con had booked for a late breakfast. Several people looked at them as they ate the set meal and talked to each other.

"I've never seen any of these people, before," whispered Blythe.

"They're just people," Con whispered back.

"They're looking at us."

"And you're looking at them. And why are we whispering."

"It seems more polite."

They didn't talk much otherwise, but the eggs were good, and there was butter with the bread. Con had chosen the place for its proximity to the district line and because it was open on Sundays. He knew that it was a longer walk after breakfast than before, and he wanted Blythe to be relaxed, to give her a break before the second leg of the journey.

They were sitting opposite each other, across a narrow table, so were physically closer than they were used to being, and facing each other.

"I'd never noticed before," said Blythe. "Your eyes are an extraordinary colour."

"They're hazel," said Con.

"I always thought they were brown, but, up close they really are a rich, dark hazel colour."

"Yours are brown. Like bottomless... somethings..."

"So, you're not good with metaphor... Odd for such an avid reader," said Blythe, smiling. "I got a lot of physical traits from my donor: The yellow skin, black hair, short stature."

"Me, too."

"What's that about?"

"What?"

"Your tone. You sound, I don't know... Sad, maybe angry."

"We can talk about it on the way, if you're finished?"

"I am, thank you."

They held their ids up to the scanner in the booth to pay for their meals, then left the lunch bar.

Blythe took a deep breath, relieved to be out of the strange environment.

"So, why the tone?" she asked again.

Con started walking, and Blythe jogged a few steps to catch up with him.

"You really want to know?" he asked.

"Only if you don't mind talking about it."

"No, I don't mind," said Con. "Your mother was white?"

"Yes. How did you know?"

"You said you take after your donor."

"You said that you do too."

"It's one of the reasons my mother didn't like me," said Con. "Probably, the biggest single reason."

"But it must have been a good genetic match for resistance," said Blythe. "Isn't that the point? We're healthier than any generation before us, less susceptible to inherited conditions, with better immune systems. We don't get sick as much as they did."

"That *is* the point, but it's worth remembering that we're the first generation of global matching."

"There have been people of many races here for hundreds of years."

"Well, apparently, my mother didn't know any of them, and, if she did, she didn't like any of them."

"Your mother was a… She was a…"

"My mother was a racist," said Con.

"How is that even possible?" asked Blythe. "That's almost beyond belief… I mean, I know, historically… I don't know how you can even say that word, especially about your mother."

"I can say it, because it's true. I don't know what she expected, but she always told me that I wasn't the child she wanted. She hated the colour of my skin, and the kinkiness of my hair. She used to shave my head when I was a child."

"I just don't get it," said Blythe.

"Me neither," said Con.

"But you were her child!" said Blythe. "And you're beautiful."

Con bowed his head, and began to walk a little faster.

Blythe skipped to keep up.

"I'm sorry, what did I say to upset you? I didn't mean to."

Concord stopped, and looked at Blythe.

"No one's ever told me that I'm beautiful, before," he said.

They regarded each other for a long moment.

"This way," said Con, heading down a path to the left.

They didn't talk for almost half an hour.

"What do you think this was like, before?" asked Blythe.

"How do you mean?"

They were walking along an old road that had once been tarmac, but the surface had broken up, there were potholes, and plants were growing through large cracks. Pieces of paving stones, from the old footpaths were broken and dislodged, trees growing through and between them, and the land on either side was divided into plots that people were tending.

"You think these old roads were used, once upon a time?" asked Blythe. "They look like the roads and paths at home, but left to rot."

"We're following one of the old roads on my map," said Con. "I guess it was built here for a reason, but it has no use any more. It's just a track to follow that takes us to where we're going."

"And this is how we avoid the quarantine wipe?"

"This track runs parallel to the transport artery. I'm pretty sure we've already passed the wipe."

"We've crossed the district line?" asked Blythe.

"If I'm right about our pace," said Con, checking his watch, "and the distance we've walked since breakfast, then, yes, we've crossed the district line."

"Without even knowing it?" asked Blythe.

"Without even knowing it!"

"Are you ever going to tell me where we're going?"

"Since we're past halfway, and since we've cleared the wipe, I'll tell you which district we're heading for. How's that?"

"I'm ready."

"We're heading for BRd1," said Con, smiling.

"No we're not!"

She stopped, suddenly, in the middle of the deserted road. She put her hands on her hips, and glared in Con's direction.

Con turned to look at her.

"What do you mean, 'no we're not'?" asked Con.

"If I wanted to go to BRd1, I could've arranged transport, and been assigned a route. It wouldn't be the first time."

"Why would you ever go to BRd1? I don't understand."

"Don't lie to me, Concord Penn," said Blythe, still glaring, her face flushed. "You planned this all along, didn't you?"

"Well," said Con, staying a couple of metres away from the fierce little woman. "Yes, I did have a plan, but I had no idea that you'd been to BRd1 before, and I have no idea why you think I've brought you here."

"My mother's been nagging me for months to visit her, and I've been avoiding it… You know I've been avoiding it."

"What has this got to do with your mother? I don't know anything about your mother, except what you've told me."

"So you're not taking me to see my mother?" asked Blythe.

"Why would I do that? I know all about mothers, and I totally respect your relationship with yours. If you want to see her, that's up to you, and if you don't, I'm the last person who'd make you."

"Why would you bring me to BRd1, if not to visit my mother?"

"Wait. Are you telling me that your mother lives in BRd1?"

"Of course," said Blythe, "why else would I think you'd tricked me into visiting her?"

"It's purely a coincidence, I promise you."

"What sort of coincidence makes you plan a visit to the place where my mother lives?"

"A very weird sort of coincidence."

"You and weird seem to be very close friends."

"Apparently," said Con. "Can we keep going? I promise you it'll all be worth it."

"It had bloody better be," said Blythe. "Otherwise, I might never forgive you, Concord Penn."

"Of course you will," he said, smiling. "You think I'm beautiful."

Nik Abnett

In less than an hour, Con and Blythe were in more familiar territory. They had entered the outskirts of the district, with its closely packed, familiar looking streets, with proper roads and unbroken pavements.

"It's not very different from SEd6, is it?" asked Con.

"Not very different at all," said Blythe. "What were you expecting?"

"Honestly? I didn't know what to expect; I've never set foot out of my own district."

"No," said Blythe. "I'd forgotten."

"How are your feet?"

"They're okay. I wouldn't mind sitting down for a while, sometime soon, though."

"Good," said Con, "and I'm hoping that'll be doable."

"Hoping? I thought I was on a promise. You said you knew exactly where we were going. I hope I haven't walked all this way for nothing."

"I'm sure it'll be doable."

"How are your feet?"

"They're sore. I think my pinky toe's about to drop off. I can't wait to get my shoes off."

"Good," said Blythe. "It serves you right."

Five minutes later, Con stopped outside a building.

"I think this is it," he said.

"It's apartments. Why have we come to some strange apartment building, miles from home?"

"Just scan your id, and see if you can get in."

"Are you sure?"

"Trust me."

Blythe held her id up to the scanner, and the exterior door opened. Con gave her a gentle push into the wipe. The doors closed, and he couldn't see her any more, but he was afraid for her, so he took a step closer to the doors, and waited.

Three or four seconds later, the doors opened again. Con expected to see Blythe in the wipe, but she wasn't there. He could see her inside the lobby, beyond the acrylic interior doors.

Con glanced quickly left and right, and then walked into the wipe. The exterior doors closed behind him, and he smelled geraniums. He expected the exterior doors to open and let him back out into the street. Instead, the interior door opened, allowing him access to the lobby. He stepped through.

"What happened?" asked Blythe.

"I don't know," said Con.

"How did we get in?"

"You got in because of your genetic coding," said Con. "This is where your cousin Dharma lives."

Blythe folded at the waist, and then her knees went too, so that she was half-crouching, half-squatting, her head between her knees.

"Are you okay?" asked Con.

"Mm,"

"Talk to me, Blythe, are you okay?"

Blythe lifted her head a little.

"I'm okay. It's just… It's all a bit of a shock, that's all."

"It was meant to be a surprise," said Con. "A nice one."

"It is," said Blythe. She straightened her knees, still bent over. "Just give me a minute."

"Of course, Dharma's data was good, but this was the only way to prove that the two of you are related. It's good news."

Blythe said nothing.

Con stood in the lobby, only a metre away from her, while she recovered. He hadn't expected the reaction, and he still wasn't sure whether he'd done a good thing.

Eventually Blythe stood upright, and her breathing steadied.

"You're okay?" asked Con.

"I'm fine," said Blythe. "Excited, but okay."

"Okay," said Con. "Good."

"There is just one thing, though…"

"All right," said Con, wary.

"If I got through the wipe because of my genetic coding, how did you get through?"

"I don't know," said Con. "I can only guess that it's faulty. I was standing very close to the door, in case you came straight out and needed me. I was a bit scared when those solid doors closed, and I couldn't see you, what you were doing…"

"You think you got some of my code on you, and the wipe read it?" asked Blythe.

"Technically," said Con, "that's possible. We've been in each other's company for a few hours, and we haven't been through a wipe since the lunch bar."

"That'll be it, then."

"Yes, that'll be it," Con agreed.

Forty-nine

Dharma was in her living room, putting more of the genealogical data in order, when the buzzer sounded.

She hadn't heard the buzzer go off in her apartment, ever. That wasn't true, she'd heard it sound twice before. On both occasions it had been to allow maintenance workers into her home.

Dharma froze. She decided to ignore it. She sat motionless for ten or fifteen seconds. The buzzer sounded again.

Whoever it was, they didn't want to leave her alone.

Dharma thought about what to do. She felt safe in her apartment, but she didn't feel safe allowing visitors in when she didn't know who they were or what they wanted. The lobby would be safer.

She didn't know how long she'd been thinking about what to do next, when the buzzer sounded yet again.

No one could get into the apartment, except for Dharma. The locks were set to her exact genetic code. The only way someone could get in was if she invited them in. Yes, the lobby was safer.

Dharma pulled on a jacket, as if she was going out. She closed the door behind her and walked down the stairs. She felt a little breathless, and decided that was just anxiety. She'd never had any problems with the stairs before.

Once she was out of the flat, it was impossible for Dharma to know whether she was being buzzed, again.

She walked slowly down the last flight of stairs, hoping the lobby would be empty when she got there.

A man and a woman were standing a couple of metres inside the interior door. She did not recognise them. They must live in the block, though, because there was no way to get into the lobby without a genetic code... It was more basic than the scanner for her front door, more universal, but you had to try a lot of doors before you'd get through one on a technicality.

Dharma decided to walk past them, as if she was going out for something.

As she approached them, she realised that the little woman was looking at her... staring even.

Dharma kept facing forwards, avoiding eye contact.

"You!" said the woman as Dharma passed her.

Dharma turned, slowly, and took a step back so that she'd be closer to the wipe, and an escape route, if she needed one.

"Can I help you?" she asked.

"Look at her,"the stranger said to her companion.

"You!" the woman said to Dharma. "Look at him!"

She did.

"I'm sorry," she said, "I don't know you... either of you."

"Give me your id."

"I can't do that!" said Dharma.

"No, I'm sorry, of course you can't." She turned back to the man. "Read your donor number out loud to her."

"What?"

"Just do it. Look at your donor number while he reads his out," she told Dharma.

"I don't need to look at it. I know it."

The man read his id out, as instructed. "5JV2012Ng."

Dharma felt faint. She leaned against the acrylic doors of the wipe and allowed herself to slide down until she was sitting on the floor.

"Breathe. It's better if you breathe."

Dharma closed her eyes, and tried to suck air in through her nose. It took an enormous effort. Her head felt light, and her chest felt as if something heavy had landed on it suddenly.

"Just keep breathing. I probably should have told you to sit down before he read the code. I'm sorry. You've had a shock."

"Yes," said Dharma. "I've had a shock." She gasped for breath, open-mouthed. "It's... I don't know what to say."

"Don't say anything," said the woman. "Just sit there and breathe. It's okay... You'll be okay."

She turned to her friend. "You'd better sit down, too."

He looked back and forth between the two of them. "I don't get it. What's going on?"

"Obviously," said the woman, "when I saw her walking across the lobby I thought you'd lied to me. I thought we were here for her. But then you didn't seem to recognise her. It's all just the most amazing coincidence. You really should sit down."

He walked to the lobby wall, a little further away, to give the woman some space, and sat down with his back against it, his legs stretched out in front of him.

"How are you doing?" the woman asked, turning back to Dharma.

"Better. A little confused, but better."

"Good. Do you think you can read your donor number out, so he can hear it?" she asked.

"I think so," said Dharma. She closed her eyes while she said it, slowly, "2JV2012Ng" she said.

There was silence for several seconds, then the young man said. "That's one digit difference."

"The first digit is for the number of live births," said Dharma. "The rest is the unique identifier for the donor."

"Yes. What made you –?"

"It explains how you got into the building," the woman said. "And, you look exactly alike! Same colouring, same hair, same gait even. I bet if I got up close to her, she'd have the same colour eyes as you, too."

"They're hazel," said Dharma, "but dark."

"Told you."

"What are the odds?" she said to the man, evidently excited by the mad coincidence. "You're good with numbers."

"Outliers," said Dharma. "Nobody moves, since the Deluge... Outliers, but inside the parameters."

"We didn't come for me," said the man. "Blythe! This was supposed to be about you!" Dharma gasped, registering the name. "I found your cousin Dharma... You were going to meet your cousin Dharma."

Dharma struggled for another breath.

217

Nik Abnett

"It's okay," said Blythe. "Just stay there and keep breathing. You'll be okay. I promise. I'm sorry you've had a shock, but it's a good one… Isn't it?"

Everyone was silent for a minute or two, partly because no one knew what to say, and partly because Dharma was still having some problems getting her head around all this.

Finally, the colour began to come back to the older woman's cheeks, the golden brown tone, returning.

"Outliers," she said again. "Beyond the statistical norm, but outliers… There's maths…"

There were a few more moments of silence.

"Sit down, Blythe," the woman then said, sounding stronger. "And take your own advice and breathe."

Blythe hesitated but then sat down as instructed. She was still excited for Con and this stranger. She had never known anyone who had a half-sibling, or who had met a half-sibling. She thought about Dharma and their relationship, and how important it had become to her. If she could feel this way about a cousin, how must Con and this woman feel about each other?

"If you're Blythe," said the woman. "Can I assume that this is Concord?" She gestured at her half-brother.

"How do you know my name?" asked Con.

She kept her eyes on Blythe.

"I know Concord's name because I'm Dharma Tuke, and you're my cousin, Blythe Dole."

Fifty

"How do you use all this space?" asked Con, as he sat down in Dharma's living room, and looked around.

"You don't have a more pressing question?" asked Blythe.

"There's plenty of time to talk," said Dharma. "To answer your question, Con. I've got used to the space. I've lived here for a while. I took an upper floor apartment to be close to my mother when she went into senior housing. It was the best way to ensure that we stayed in the same district, so I could visit her at weekends."

"You were close to your mother?" asked Con.

"Very, I think," said Dharma. "She's really the reason I wanted to connect to Blythe."

"You wanted family?" asked Blythe.

"I've been alone a long time, and I've never known how to make friends, so I thought that blood mattered. It mattered to my mother. She spoke often of my grandmother."

"Your grandmother was Blythe's grandmother's sister," said Con.

"That's right. I didn't know my mother had an aunt. She never mentioned her, so perhaps she didn't know, either."

"The Deluge broke families up," said Con.

Blythe was still standing, beside the table where Dharma ate, and worked on her family trees.

"Have a seat, Blythe," said Dharma. "I could make some tea."

"I was just looking at the geraniums," said Blythe.

"Oh," said Dharma. "You know what they are?"

"My mother's senior housing has a garden. It's lovely. My mother insists on walking around it almost every day. When she's not complaining that I don't spend enough time with her, she's talking about the garden."

"Something else we have in common. My mother kept a window box at her senior housing. I never took much interest."

"Neither did I, but when I go to see her she walks me around the garden, telling me the names of all the plants, flowers especially."

"I picked those in the garden yesterday."

"Which garden?" asked Con.

"The garden at my mother's senior housing," said Dharma. "Why?"

"I thought your mother had died," said Con.

"Two years ago."

"Then how do you access the grounds?"

"My id still works. I guess I just haven't been taken out of the system yet."

"After two years!" said Con.

"I thought it was odd, and Patience asked me about it, too."

"I think I will sit down," said Blythe, taking a seat at the other end of the sofa from where Con was sitting.

"I'll go and make that tea," said Dharma. "You look like you need it."

"How do I tell her?" Blythe asked Con, when Dharma was out of earshot.

"I don't know. She's had the biggest shock of her life, today, so maybe this one won't seem so dramatic... Did it seem dramatic to you?"

"No, not really. It's all a bit odd, though, isn't it?"

"It was that name, Patience, that made you put two and two together, wasn't it?"

"It's the name of the gardener at Mum's housing," said Blythe. "I guess you got it from the genetic id code?"

"And because I know that your mum lives in senior housing in this district."

"There are several senior housing units in any given district."

"There are, but I'm beginning to think that these things aren't coincidental. I'm wondering if the State makes more choices than we realise... Manipulates us more."

"We'll tell her, though, right?" asked Blythe.

"I think we should," said Con. "She went looking for family, and now we can give her another little piece of it."

Dharma returned with a tray that had three large cups of tea on it.

"Lucky I have three mugs," she said. "I don't need three, just for me, but my kitchen seemed so empty that I bought more of everything when I moved in."

"Me too," said Blythe. "I live on the sixth floor."

"And, now that I've seen this place, I'm definitely going to apply for relocation," said Con. "I'm hoping to have visitors from time to time, now that we all have each other."

"Which brings me to something else," said Blythe. "Now that you're sitting down, Dharma."

"Not more revelations?" said Dharma.

"It's a bit of a surprise," said Con.

"I've had the surprise of my life, today," said Dharma. "I think I can handle it."

"My mother's still alive," said Blythe.

"I assumed as much," said Dharma. "There's no death record for her."

"Okay," said Blythe. "You mentioned someone called Patience, at your mother's housing."

"She's the gardener, there," said Dharma. "I liked her."

"Me, too," said Blythe.

Dharma frowned for a moment. "Liberty Dole," she finally said.

"She calls herself Libby," said Blythe.

"That's what Patience calls her, too," said Dharma.

"That's why your id still works, there," said Con.

"My mother was in the same housing as her cousin, and she never knew it?"

"It seems so. Maybe you two could visit Blythe's mother, together."

"I'd love that," said Dharma, smiling, suddenly.

"That might change," said Blythe. "You haven't met my mother."

"Don't be so hard on her," said Dharma.

"You've said that before. Do you know something that I don't know?"

Dharma talked about Liberty for a little while. She was cautious. She was a high-ranking, trusted member of the team at W.W. and she'd signed non-disclosure documents. This was different, though; this was her family. This was blood.

Blythe cried a little, and Dharma and Con tried to comfort her.

"Why didn't she tell me about it?" asked Blythe. "Things could have been different."

"Mothers have their own things," said Con, "their secrets and lies... Like most people. We can only ever know what they want to tell us."

"Would you visit my mother with me, some time?" asked Blythe.

"Of course," said Dharma.

Blythe dried her tears, and wiped her face with her hands.

"The bathroom's over there," said Dharma, "to the left. Why don't you go and splash some water on your face?"

"Thanks," said Blythe, getting up. "I think I will."

"You're a data analyst," said Con. "What do you make of all these coincidences?"

"That they're not coincidences. I'd never thought about it before, but hypotheses have been developing pretty quickly in my mind during the past couple of hours."

"It's engineered," said Con. "By the State."

"It has to be," said Dharma.

"But why?" asked Con.

"Those are the most complicated questions. Motivation is a difficult thing to work out from data, even if you know what you're looking at."

"But you have theories. It has to do with the Deluge, doesn't it?"

"And with the lack of mobility of the population," said Dharma. "Nobody moves, and nobody has moved since the Deluge."

"But for so many of us to be related, and without knowing it?"

"It's pragmatic," said Dharma, "at least, that's my guess."

"You're talking about genetic diversity?" asked Con.

"Think about who survived the Deluge."

"Family groups, who had strong leaders, and were prepared to follow the quarantine rules," said Con.

"What if the strongest of those leaders didn't just influence their immediate family members, but also influenced members at a distance. So one effective leader might have been able to influence dozens of family members over several generations."

"I suppose that's possible," said Con.

"That would constrict the gene pool dramatically, during an event like the Deluge."

Blythe walked into the wipe, and stood for a moment. She looked at the canister in its bracket, most of the aluminium can visible.

The door to the bathroom slid open, but Blythe didn't pass through it. She stood in the wipe, tilting her head so that she could read what was on the can.

She knew that alphanumeric. She knew it like she knew her own id number. She had keyed that number into invoice templates thousands of times in the past three years.

Blythe had seen plenty of wipe canisters before; she even kept a spare for her own bathroom wipe. Of the dozens of canisters she'd used at home, she'd never seen one with a number on it.

Anley Corp was in the wipe business, and Blythe had never known it. She wondered what Con knew.

Finally, Blythe walked into the bathroom and closed the door behind her. As she used the toilet, washed her hands, and splashed water on her face, she kept thinking about the canister. She was conflicted. She wanted to get to know Dharma, and she wanted to discuss her family. She wanted to give Dharma and Concord some time to talk, too; their blood tie was closer than hers to Dharma, but, somehow, she wasn't as jealous as she had been when she thought they were just friends.

Con looked up as Blythe walked back into the living room.

"What is it?" he asked.

"It's nothing. You've got more important things to talk about."

"We were only talking data," said Dharma, "and you've clearly got something on your mind. You look distracted."

"It's your bathroom wipe, that's all," said Blythe.

"You don't like the scent?" asked Dharma.

223

Nik Abnett

"Con," said Blythe. "Anley Corp is in the wipe business, isn't it?"

"It is," said Con. "How did you find out?"

"The alphanumeric on the canister in Dharma's wipe... I've keyed in that code thousands of times."

"What of it?" asked Dharma.

"Why would it be a secret?" asked Blythe. "Why isn't Anley Corp transparent about what it does?"

Con took a deep breath, and then said, "It's a front. You actually work for the government."

"Then so do you," said Blythe.

"Yes, I do," said Con.

"And why didn't you tell me? No, don't answer that. It's because you're ninetieth percentile, isn't it?"

"Those non-disclosure documents you signed," said Con. "Mine were much more rigorous."

"So you won't tell me?" asked Blythe.

"I don't know."

"You should," said Dharma. "I used confidential data to find my cousin, and you circumvented the travel restrictions to bring her here... We've also been speculating about the State."

"So, you think we've passed a point of no return?" asked Con.

"You and I have," said Dharma. "It doesn't seem fair to keep Blythe in the dark. She's one of us."

"Blood," said Con.

"That too," said Dharma, "but there's an intellectual connection, now. We shouldn't have any secrets, blood or not."

"There's some stuff you probably don't know, either, Dharma."

"And there's stuff that we've been speculating about, so the more data we share, the closer we can get to understanding our own lives."

"Fair point," said Con. "The wipes, we're all told what they're for."

"To keep us safe," said Blythe.

"And how do you suppose they do that?" asked Con.

"Fumigation," said Dharma. "That's what they were set up for. That much, I do know."

224

"That *is* what they were set up for, but that was a long time ago."

"There use has changed, over time?" asked Blythe.

"And that's why they're run by the State," said Con.

"Whatever it is they're used for now, are they universal?" asked Dharma. "The scent varies."

"The scent is just an additive," said Con, "although, different scents are used for different purposes. The flower scents, geranium, lavender, rose, are used to support relaxation, so that we don't all go crazy living alone."

"No generation before the Deluge ever lived alone," said Dharma. "Everyone lived in family groups."

"The scent is part of that, along with some low-level, mood altering drugs."

"But we're the least medicalised community of any since the birth of medicine," said Dharma.

"We are the least medicalised for cures, and the most medicalised for prevention of illness," said Con. "The wipe is a complex combination of chemicals. Some of those chemicals ensure mental wellbeing, some physical wellbeing."

"For example?" asked Blythe.

"For example, all new or unknown pathogens are isolated, grown in large numbers, and introduced into selected wipes."

"For people to get sick!" said Blythe.

"Immunisation trials," said Con. "When the data's collected, it's analysed, and a global immunisation stratagem is worked out."

"We're exposed to things that could kill us? I thought we were being fumigated! I thought I was being kept safe."

"You are," said Con. "You're immune from every current pathogen known to man."

"So I'm actually healthier because of the diseases I'm exposed to?" asked Blythe.

"It's a method that's been used for hundreds of years," said Dharma, "but I assumed that was all in the past."

"The first smallpox vaccine was developed in 1798, by a man called Edward Jenner," said Con. "In 1999, smallpox had been eradicated, globally."

"That's two hundred years!" said Blythe.

"We work a lot faster, now."

"How do you know all this?" asked Dharma.

"I'm a theoretical immunologist," said Con.

"What does that mean?" asked Blythe.

"It means that chemists and microbiologists give me scenarios, and I plot them and analyse the data," said Con.

"On your own?" asked Dharma.

"I specialise in genetic resilience in particular communities."

"I don't know if I can get my head around this," said Blythe.

"I'm working to keep us safe, and well," said Con.

"It's the Deluge effect again, isn't it?" said Dharma. "The medical costs of treating people who were going to die."

"The medical costs of keeping anyone alive, with any condition. Genetic compatibility and wipe immunisation has made prevention both better, and cheaper than any cure."

"So we're healthy," said Dharma, "and, excepting accidents, we live long lives."

"That's about the size of it," said Con. "Which brings us back to our earlier conversation."

"I don't know if I understand this conversation, completely," said Blythe. "I mean I get the gist, but... Wow!"

"It's a long walk home," said Con, smiling. "We'll talk about it some more, then."

"Okay. So what was the other conversation you were having?"

"We were saying that none of the coincidences we've talked about today are actual coincidences," said Dharma. "We're talking about how the gene pool was decimated by the Deluge. We were speculating that a relatively small number of family groups make up the biggest percentage of survivors."

"Hence the need for population control," said Con.

"I don't get it," said Blythe.

"Selecting genetic matches for procreation ensures that the gene pool grows and is more healthy. People with similar genetic backgrounds show greater incidence of inherited disease through the generations."

"But nobody moves," said Blythe.

"That's the point. After the Deluge, it was proven that the movement of people was a massive contributor to the demise of the planet. Genetically, it was important that people move out of their communities to find diverse matches for procreation."

"Those two things contradict each other," said Blythe.

"Which is why we no longer live in family groups," said Dharma.

"It's why women are offered donor matches if they want to raise a child," said Con.

"I've worked on genetic matching for a sperm bank," said Dharma. "Markers are checked so that there is, in effect, no match. When we find that the mother and the donor have genetic markers in common, those matches are discarded."

"Which is why I look like me, and you look like you, but we're related," said Blythe.

"It's the healthiest way to have a relatively small population."

"And it's why my mother rejected me," said Con, "and why 'racist' was a word that you couldn't bear to say."

"That doesn't explain you and Con, though, does it?" asked Blythe.

"Actually, it does. Nobody moves and, although we live in different districts, we live relatively close to each other. Donors don't move either, and their donations don't travel far."

"It hadn't crossed my mind before," said Con, "but we probably all see people we're related to, all of the time; we just don't know it."

"The State doesn't want us to know," said Dharma. "People who form large groups have more power to question, to protest and to lobby."

"I don't understand 'protest' or 'lobby'," said Blythe.

"Old concepts," said Dharma, "but I'm willing to bet that if we all knew all of our blood connections, we'd start to form the sort of large groups that affected governments in previous centuries."

"What do we do about all this?" asked Blythe.

"Nothing," said Con and Dharma together.

"Nothing? You spent all that time and energy looking for me, and you and Con plotted, and Con made me walk here… And, we all have each other, now… And you think we should do *nothing*?"

"We all have each other now," said Dharma. "What more could we possibly want?"

"I don't know," said Blythe.

"And neither do I," said Dharma.

"Nor me."

"You're in the ninetieth percentile, both of you, and you don't think there's more?" asked Blythe.

"We know there's no healthier way to live," said Dharma. "We know that everyone is housed, that everyone has what they need, and that everyone is happy."

"We've improved immunity, and mental health, and eradicated dozens of infectious and contagious diseases."

"And we have no families," said Blythe.

"We have each other," said Dharma.

"Yes, we do," said Blythe. "But, what about everybody else, what do they have?"

About the Author

Nik Abnett is a writer of short stories and novels, and has consulted on writing for games. Her first independent novel *Savant* was published in 2016, and was well-received. She lives and works at home with her husband, the writer Dan Abnett. She likes to knit blankets and throw pots on the wheel, and she's a good shot with a 2.2 rifle.

The Wipe was begun on 12th March 2020, the first day of her Covid lockdown. She remains in lockdown to this day, 1st January 2021.

NP NOVELLAS

An exciting new series of high calibre fiction in concentrated narratives from some of the most accomplished writers around.

#1: Universal Language – Tim Major (April 2021)

An intriguing murder mystery that pays homage to Asimov's seminal robot stories and also to the classic detective tale.

Investigator Abbey Oma is dispatched to a remote and failing Martian colony tasked with solving the murder of scientist Jerem Ferrer. The killing took place in an airlock-sealed lab, and the only possible culprit is a robot incapable of harming humans...

#2: Worldshifter – Paul Di Filippo (April 2021)

A high-octane tale reminiscent of Jack Vance at his best in its sweep and imagination, but wholly Di Filippo in its execution. When lowly shipbreaker Klom stumbles upon an active organic stasis pod deep within the bowels of a derelict ship, little does he imagine the deadly danger it represents. Klom is forced into a desperate chase across the stars as the most powerful beings in the galaxy determine to claim the secrets he has unwittingly discovered.

#3: May Day – Emma Coleman (May 2021)

Abruptly orphaned during wartime, May is forced to move to the country to live with her strict church-going aunt, who never approved of May's mum nor her heathen ways. Despite Aunt Celia's disapproval, May continues to practice the superstitions her mum drummed into her, until the one time she doesn't, at which point something dark arises and proceeds to invade her life...

www.newconpress.co.uk